Coke Kings

Lock Down Publications and Ca$h
Presents
Coke Kings
A Novel by *T.J. Edwards*

Coke Kings

Lock Down Publications
P.O. Box 870494
Mesquite, Tx 75187

Visit our website @
www.lockdownpublications.com

Copyright 2019 Coke Kings

First Edition June 2019
Printed in the United States of America

This is a work of fiction. Names, characters, places, and incidents either are products of the author's imagination or are used fictitiously. Any similarity to actual events or locales or persons, living or dead, is entirely co-incidental.

Lock Down Publications
Like our page on Facebook: Lock Down Publications @
www.facebook.com/lockdownpublications.ldp
Cover design and layout by: **Dynasty Cover Me**
Book interior design by: **Shawn Walker**
Edited by: **Lashonda Johnson**

3

Stay Connected with Us!

Text **LOCKDOWN** to 22828 to stay up-to-date with
new releases, sneak peaks, contests and more…

Thank you.

Submission Guideline.

Submit the first three chapters of your completed manuscript to ldpsubmissions@gmail.com, subject line: Your book's title. The manuscript must be in a .doc file and sent as an attachment. Document should be in Times New Roman, double spaced and in size 12 font. Also, provide your synopsis and full contact information. If sending multiple submissions, they must each be in a separate email.

Have a story but no way to send it electronically? You can still submit to LDP/Ca$h Presents. Send in the first three chapters, written or typed, of your completed manuscript to:

LDP: Submissions Dept
Po Box 870494
Mesquite, Tx 75187

DO NOT send original manuscript. Must be a duplicate.

Provide your synopsis and a cover letter containing your full contact information.

Thanks for considering LDP and Ca$h Presents.

T.J. Edwards

6

Chapter 1

Kammron stood in front of the full-length mirror and flicked a piece of lint off his Gucci jeans, before tucking his black wife beater inside them. He slid on the black and red Gucci top that would offset his matching retro number eleven Jordan's.

He grabbed his gold-framed Gucci glasses off the dresser and smiled. "That's a muthafuckin' Boss, right there," he mused.

Shelly waltzed into the room with her arms folded across her chest. She stared at him for a moment and sighed, "So, I guess you're going to Jimmy's party anyway? I thought we was gon' chill and watch this *'Love Me Even When It Hurts'* movie?"

Kammron sat on the edge of the bed and fit his feet into his Jordan's one at a time. He stood up, and pulled on the tongue, then tucked the pants behind them. "Yo, later for all that soft movie watching shit. My word, every time we watch them joints you get to crying and acting all emotional and shit. We just did that whole gig three days ago. I can only sign up for that once a week, and even then, it's a stretch." He shook his head and stood back in front of the mirror.

Kammron was six-feet even, weighed a hundred and eighty-five pounds, had caramel-skinned with a low cut, deep waves, and brown eyes.

He stared at her by use of her reflection in the mirror. "What the fuck you looking all stupid for?"

She smacked her lips. "Yo, who da fuck you talking to, Kamm?"

"I'm talking to you, every time you see a nigga getting fitted and shit you get to making them crazy looking ass faces.

7

So, I'ma ask you again. What the fuck are you looking all stupid for?" He could feel himself becoming vexed.

Shelly had been his li'l dame ever since their tenth-grade year. Kammron had knocked her after she was voted the most baddest bitch in school by their peers that were smashing. Never been one to settle for less, after that title for her came out he just had to have her. The pursuit took less than two months, then it took an additional month for him to hit that ass. All in all, in his opinion he felt she was a good girl, and worthy to be called his main, Bitch. There was way too much pussy in the world for him to consider her his only one. That thought was almost comical to him.

Shelly was a dark-skinned Puerto Rican. Five-feet-six inches tall, a hundred and thirty pounds, with dark brown eyes, and curly hair that fell to the center of her back.

"Nah, it's just that it's cool for you to hit up parties all over Harlem, and shit. But you want me to stay in this house all day long, every single day. That shit ain't fair and you know it." She plopped on the bed. This caused her short nightgown to rise on her thick thighs. He could see a hint of her pink lace panties underneath. "Shid, I wanna go out sometimes, too. What you don't think that I like to have fun or something?"

Kammron threw his gold rope around his neck, took his Glock out of the top drawer and slid it into the small of his back. "Shorty, you can do whatever the fuck you wanna do. We only eighteen, I ain'tcha mafuckin' daddy. I ain't trying to stand on you about nothing." He turned around to face her. "How is a nigga looking?"

She winced in emotional aggravation. "Ugly!" she lied.

She hated him for being so damn fine. Harlem was known for dressing, and it was no secret that when it came to dressing, Kammron did his thing. He took looking good personal it seemed to her.

Kammron laughed. "Bitch you just hating. You know a mafucka looking good as a fifty-million-dollar winning lottery ticket. My swag terrific." He faced the mirror again. "Yo, I'm fa real, though. If you wanna get up out of the house, I'm cool wit' that. You too young to be cramped up in here all day and night anyway. It's the summer, enjoy that shit."

Shelly walked behind him and laid her face on his shoulder. "Ain't nothing out here for me, Kamm, especially not at no party. Everything I'm looking for is right here in front of me." She stepped around him and stood in his face.

She wrapped her arms around his neck. Her pretty, brown eyes peered into his. Her eyelashes were naturally long and added to her beauty.

"Can I get some of my man before you go out then?" Shelly felt that if she drained Kammron before he left the house than she ran the shorter risk of him cheating on her with one of the many Free throws of Harlem.

Harlem had females that were so aggressive, and only in for the night, that it made it hard for struggling faithful women like Shelly to maintain their loyalty. She took his hand and slid it down the front of her panties. Right over her freshly shaven pussy lips.

Kammron opened them up and trailed his finger in circles around her opening. His forehead rested against hers. He was already imagining what her grips would feel like. "Yo, this yo' way of seducing a nigga?" His middle finger slid in as deep as it could go.

Her lips immediately closed around it and heat suffocated the digit, her scent was *Prada's Cherry Blossoms*. She moaned and arched her back to feel him better. "I just want some dick before you go that's all. You already know how hard it is for me to get to sleep unless you put me there." She opened her thighs wider and licked her lips.

Kammron leaned his head all the way back, and took a deep breath, as he stared at the ceiling. "Yo, you get me like this every time. You already know you ain't gon' be able to handle this dick once I get all up in that ass. You still got that baby pussy ma, word." He slipped a second finger into her box and worked them in and out. His dick was harder than a drive-by shooter.

"Unn—killa, I'm getting better, you'll see." She unbuckled his belt and forced them down his thighs. Then dropped to her knees, and grabbed his penis in her little fist, pumping it. "I want this, Papi. I want you to fuck me wit' this, right here. Your baby needs it." She kissed the head and licked circles around it, then sucked him into her mouth. "Mmm!"

Kammron closed his eyes and humped into her mouth slowly. Her tongue play was on point. Her fist was tight enough to drive him nuts as she pumped him.

"Yo, fuck—suck, Papi then, Mami. Handle ya bidness."

His short strokes turned into long ones. He grabbed a handful of her curly hair and guided her back and forth.

Shelly sucked faster, her tongue flicked up and down his hole, then she was sucking on the head like a vacuum cleaner. She felt that if she could get him to cum at least twice then there was a chance he wouldn't even leave her mother's house, let alone go out to find some random free throw to sleep with. It was like her mother had said if she wanted to keep her man in the house, she needed to keep him drained.

Kammron backed into the wall and closed his eyes tight. Her wet, hot lips were going into overdrive. He groaned and fucked her face faster. Then pulled back with his piece throbbing in the air shining from her saliva.

"Yo, I wanna fuck something, get ya ass up." He pulled her up by the hair and pressed her against the wall.

Then he leaned his face into her neck, and bit into it, before sucking hard. His hand was between her thighs, searching until he found her slippery pussy. The lips felt hot and spongy. Shelly moaned and stroked his dick fast. It poked at her stomach. She stood on tippy toe, and guided the head into her opening, then humped forward and slowly but surely, she began to engulf him.

"Uhhhhhhhh."

Kammron picked her up by her ass and plunged deep. Her back landed against the wall as he made her rise and fall on his piece. "Fuck, Mami!"

"Uh-uh-uh-uh-uh—wait, Papi!" She wrapped her thighs around his waist and licked all over his neck. Her breathing was labored as her mouth opened wide. "Uhhhhhhhh—Papi! Papi-uh-uh, yes."

Kammron ripped the top of her gown to expose her succulent breasts. They came spilling out, the nipples were chocolate brown and erect. He fell to the bed with her still attached and his piece ran in and out of her at full speed. Her legs wrapped around his waist. She received him with complete bliss, and love.

"Uh-uh-uh-uh-uh—Kamm! Uh, fuck, fuck baby. It—feel—soooo—good!" she gasped, digging her nails into his sides as he pounded harder and harder. "I love you, Papi, I love youuu!"

Kammron was all focus, he clapped into her waist over and over. He watched her breasts bounce up and down on her chest. Her sex faces drove him crazy. One second, she was frowning as if she were in pain. The next a big smile spread across her face that was quickly turned back into a frown. Her eyelids squeezed tightly, while her long tongue traced her lips. He looked down and watched his chocolate dick travel in and out of her dripping pussy. Their sexual coupling created a puddle of secretions under her ass. Kammron took her right thigh and placed it on his shoulder, before biting into her neck, growling and fucking her hard.

"Arrgh."

"Papi-Papi-Papi—uuhhh, Papi! Aw shit, slow down— slow down, Papi. Shit, I'm cumming, I'm cumming—ooo!" Shelly threw her head back and moaned at the top of her lungs.

Kammron could feel her tight muscles sucking at him. Her heat seemed to intensify. He jerked and growled even louder, while licking her neck, and sucking hard on it before pulling out of her pussy, and cumming all over her stomach in globs. He pumped his piece as spurt after spurt landed on her skin.

Shelly opened her legs wide and started playing wit' her pussy. She pinched her sex lips together, and ran her finger down the center of them, before pinching her erect clitoris and sending more chills throughout her body.

Kammron finished his business and stood on the side of the bed with his piece still as hard as cement. It jumped while he watched Shelly rub his semen into her stomach.

"Damn baby." He eyed her peach. "It seems like that li'l pussy getting fatter and fatter."

Shelly opened herself with her fingers and ran her tongue across her lips. "Papi, I know you ain't done, are you?" Two fingers slipped into her box. She pulled them out and sucked them into her mouth.

Kammron continued to stroke himself. As good as her pussy looked, he knew that whenever Jimmy threw a party that it set Harlem on fire. If he wasted all his nuts bussing down with Shelly, he was less likely to perform well if he and Bonkers just so happened to run into a couple of bad Bitches from around the way.

"Papi, just give me five more minutes. I need you to hit this shit from the back." She crawled onto her knees, spaced them apart, reached under herself, and opened her lips again. All Kammron's fight left him after seeing her pose in this position. He pumped his piece a few more times, and slowly slid into her hotness again. He held her by her waist and brought her ass cheeks onto his lap. Then he started pounding her as if he was angry.

Bap! Bap! Bap! Bap!

Their skin slapped together.

Shelly laid her face on the bed, and closed her eyes, moaning with a smile on her face. She knew that after he'd cum the second time it would prevent him from making too many mistakes at the party. She loved Kammron, she felt deep within her heart of hearts that one day he was going to be her husband. She'd had one too many dreams detailing their futures for that not to be true. She would have to weather the storm as her mother would put it. Give him some time to grow up, and into her. Then he would be all hers.

Kammron smacked her hard on the ass and continued to pound her out. There was nothing like fucking a bad bitch too him, and Shelly was most definitely that. She was bad from head to tie, and he knew he had her stuck on him. He'd been the first and only nigga to ever get the pussy. Ever since the first time he'd had her under his thumb, and for him there was nothing like going into the streets and doing your dirt and knowing the whole time that you had a bad bitch waiting back at the crib for you. The feeling was like no other. He pounded her as hard as he could. Pulled her long hair and fucked her some more. She reached between her thick thighs and diddled her clit.

She screamed and came just as hard as before. Then fell to her stomach as he continued stroking her fast, and hard.

"Fuck, baby. Uh, damn, baby-fuck-fuck-arrgh-arrgh!" He pulled out again, and came all over her ass, and lower back. Then rubbed his dick head up, and down her ass crack leaving it slimy, and wet. He laid on his back, still shaking.

Shelly took his piece into her fist and squeezed it hard, bringing a drop of his semen to the top of it, and licked it off. Then she gave him some of the best after sex head she could muster, trying so desperately to provoke a third cum from him.

Kammron pushed her face off his dick. "Shorty, chill damn. You gon' break my shit. Yo', I'm done!" He scooted from under her and stood up.

She shook her head. "No, you're not, look at it. It's still hard. Come here, Papi, let me finish you off. She crawled across the bed with her titties bouncing on her chest.

Kammron waved her off. "Yo, later for all that shit, Shorty. I'm already fashionably late for the party." He stepped to the dresser and picked up his cell phone. "Yo', this nigga Bonkers been blowing me up, Kid stupid mad, right now." He replaced the phone and eased into the bathroom closing the door. "I'm finna take a quick shower, I'll be out in a minute."

Shelly felt ready to scream she was so irate. After all, they'd done, he was still set to go to the party. *Do you need any help in there?*" she yelled, masking her frustrations.

"Nah, Shorty, stay yo' ass out there, the God good!"

She laid on her back and pulled the covers over her head. She didn't know why she loved him so much, but one thing was for sure, and that was she was stuck on him and had been ever since high school.

Chapter 2

"Yo', dis how you roll up to a party, God. In a muthafuckin' twenty-nineteen Benz, sitting on twenty-eight. This bitch fresher than a juicy apple that been picked from a tree five seconds ago," Bonkers bragged, stepping out the black on black Mercedes Benz, dressed in Marc Jacobs from head to toe.

He was midnight black, with brown eyes, and a Mohawk style haircut that he kept curly at the top. He had two gold ropes around his neck, and a gold Rolex watch flooded with ice. He adjusted his pants to make sure his Glock .40 wouldn't slip out of it.

Kammron jumped out of the passenger's seat with a bottle of Ace of Spades in his right hand, and a blunt of Loud in the other between his fingers. "Yo, easy, nigga. You and I both know this boy is hot as a fat Bitch in the summer wearing a sweater. Easy nigga." He laughed and took a sip of the champagne.

Bonkers and Kammron had been best friends since they were one in daycare. Kathy, Kammron's mother said that when they went to the same daycare as kid's they'd always avoid everybody else, and only play with one another. Since daycare they'd fought together, fucked hoes together clapped niggas together, and conquered their jungle together daily. Bonkers was like Kammron's blood brother, it had always been that way.

"Yo', son, quit putting the God's bidness out there. Let a mafucka shine for a minute." He took a Dutch from behind his ear, lit it and gazed upon the crowded street.

The entire street of a hundred and forty-fifth and Lennox was jam-packed with cars, and people getting out of them headed up to Jimmy's party. Most of the cars were playing music so loud that it sounded like a concert already. There were females stepping out of their whips, pulling their way to short skirts down enough to conceal their panties or sex parts underneath. Others adjusted their tops to keep their breasts in place. It was just after eleven o'clock, on a hot summer night. The Mosquitoes were out and biting like crazy.

"Yo', one thing about, big bruh, son definitely know how to throw a party." Bonkers cheesed looking around.

He stepped up on the stoop, and one of the old heads from the hood that Jimmy had put in place as security blocked his path.

Kammron eased beside Bonkers and placed his hand under his shirt ready to wet something. "Yo,' what's really good ma, nigga?"

The old head looked him off. "Ain't nobody getting in the party wit' guns on them. Jimmy told me to pat everybody down no exceptions. I'm doing all the niggas, she doing, all the broads." He nodded his head at a female that neither man was familiar with. She was patting down one female after the next.

Bonkers mugged him. "Nigga, if you don't get the fuck out of my way, we about to have a muthafuckin' problem of epic proportions around this bitch. This my brother shit. You ain't touching me with them crusty ass hands. If you even try it, I'ma splash yo' shit all over this stoop."

This got Kammron excited. Whenever Bonkers got on some killa shit it ignited the animal in him as well.

He bumped the old head out of the way. "You heard what the fuck my nigga said, B. Get the fuck out the way." He could feel his heart beating harder than a bass drum.

The old head took a step back and held his hands at shoulder level. "Look, I'm just doing what Jimmy paid me to do.

He said don't let nobody in, those were my orders," the heavyset man said loud enough so Jimmy could hear him.

Bonkers got heated, he upped his Glock and cocked it. "Bitch, get the fuck out of the way, I ain't gon' tell you again." The old head stepped to the side. "Man, gon Bonkers, damn."

Kammron smiled. "Fuck nigga you know what dis is. You almost lost yo' life playing them dumb ass games." They stepped into the hallway and then eased into the party.

The disco lights were already flashing as music blared loudly. Kammron nodded his head and smiled. He could smell a heavy scent of perfume, weed and cigarette smoke. The party was shoulder to shoulder.

Bonkers leaned into his ear. "Yo,' kid, I was ready to smoke that, old nigga. My word, had we stood in front of that clown for three more seconds I was knocking his head off."

Kammron laughed. "If you popped him twice, I was hitting his ass three times. You already know how this shit go." He placed his hand on Bonkers' shoulder. "Yo', calm down now, Kid. It's plenty pussy in the house, let's focus on that. Plus, it gotta be plenty of capers in this mafucka. You know how, Jimmy, do."

Bonkers nodded. "You're right, let's roll, son." Bunkers eased more into the party, and pulled the arm of a short, but well put together Puerto Rican female. She'd been slow winding to the song blaring out of the speakers. "Yo,' ma, what's good?"

She smiled and shook her head. "Nothing, I'm here wit' somebody."

Bonkers squinted his eyes. "Yo, so what, I'm here now. Fuck that other nigga."

She winced in pain he was holding her wrist now incredibly tight. "Let me go, nigga, I don't know you like that."

Kammron stepped up. "Bruh, fuck shorty, she ain't even all that. Just look around the party, it's plenty bad bitches here."

Bonkers mugged Kammron for what seemed like a long time, then gradually snapped out of his zone. He pushed her back into the crowd, causing her to fall back. "Yo,' dis, Harlem son. This our shit, bitches be acting all stuck up and shit. They can catch these hot ones too, son, word to, Janine." Janine was Bonkers' mother.

Kammron laughed and watched the Puerto Rican climb to her feet. "Fuck that, bitch, Kid." He took the bottle of Ace of Spades and poured it into her hair. "Dis Harlem, bitch, me and my mans a be running this mafucka real soon, and you gon' wish you fucked wit' us niggas." He placed his arm around Bonkers' neck and strolled into the party with him.

Nearly everywhere they looked, they saw females twerking with their hands on their knees or grinding into the laps of the dope boys from the hood. Most of the niggas held bottles of expensive champagnes into the air, while they grooved with the person in front of them. It was a regular Friday night in Harlem. Both Kammron and Bonkers were accustomed to such gatherings.

When they made it to the back of the house, Jimmy stepped from the back room wearing a black beater, and a gun holster, with two Glock, .40s in each holster. "Just the two li'l niggas I have been hoping to see. I got some bidness for you young Harlem animals." Jimmy was five-feet eleven inches tall, light-skinned, with long cornrows that fell to his waist. He and Bonkers had the same mother and different fathers. Jimmy's father was a Cuban heavyweight in the dope game. His name was Ruiz. Ruiz and Jimmy had a strange relationship because of how Ruiz used to beat Janine into the ground

18

when they were kids. He never could forgive the man for his abusive ways.

Bonkers pulled his nose and sniffed hard. "I hope you got something else coupled wit' that bidness for li'l bruh. Nah, mean?"

Jimmy pulled a small package of Boy out of his pants pocket and flicked it. "Oh, you already know I got that tar baby. Y'all come in this back room, and fuck wit' me for a minute." He waved for them to follow him.

Kammron took one last look over his shoulder, before following behind Jimmy, and Bonkers. When they got into the back room, he saw that a small table had been set up back there. Up on the table was a big bottle of Patron, ten rolled Dutches, an ashtray, a broken piece of a mirror, and two rolled up fifty-dollar bills.

Bonkers took a seat at the table and placed the mirror in front of him. Jimmy handed him the package of tar, and as soon as he did, he dumped a nice portion of it on the mirror, made two lines, grabbed a rolled fifty, and took a line straight to the dome. He held that nostril closed and tilted his head back. The effects of the potent drug took its effect almost immediately. First came the bells, then the music. His body began to hum and feel numb. He cleared the second line and increased his high before the first one could settle into him.

Jimmy placed his arm around Kammron's shoulder. "What's good wit' you Kamm, you fucking wit' that dog food, too?" He watched Bonkers stretch out in the chair. He closed his eyes and frowned.

Kammron pulled his arm off him. "N'all, Kid, just hit me wit' a few Purks and the God a be good to go. I ain't graduated yet," he joked.

It seemed like everybody in Harlem was fucked up on heroin. Kammron felt like he was the last of a dying breed. He wanted to stay clear of the drug. He didn't like being addicted to anything, but especially not a drug.

Jimmy gave him two Percocets, both thirties. "Here you go li'l Homie, enjoy."

Kammron popped them and chased them with the bottle of Ace of Spade. "Yo', so what the deal? You got a move lined up for us?"

Jimmy sat at the table and made him two lines, tooted them, and pinched his nostrils together. He made a weird noise with his throat while he allowed the tar to do its job. As soon as the effects took over him, he nodded his head. "Yeah, I need y'all to make a drop-off, and a pick up for me, out in Jersey." He grabbed the bottle of Patron and turned it up.

"Yo, what the fuck you got going on out there, Kid?" Bonkers asked, finally opening his eyes. They were red as a pool ball.

"All you need to know is that you gon' be rolling this Buick Century out that way. It's gon' be this Cuban cat that's gon' check the trunk. After he comes back and gives you a head nod, one of his boys' gon' remove what's in the trunk and put a bag inside of it. It's as simple as that, the job pays five gees a piece to you li'l niggas."

Kammron stood up and stretched his arms above his head. "Yo', all I need to know is if I gotta splash some shit? How you know these Cubans ain't on no bullshit?"

Jimmy grunted. "Cause if I thought they was gon' be I wouldn't be sending you li'l niggas, I'd be sending some head bussahs. I know how to work this shit."

"Yo', fuck you saying, Dunn? You saying me and my mans don't split heads a somethin'?" Kammron asked getting vexed.

"Yeah, Jimmy, as you recall I handled my first body at eleven-years-old. Right outside of Malcolm Shabazz. Kamm was right there. He helped me pull the nigga to the tracks and everything. We been trigger happy ever since then."

Jimmy pulled at the hairs on his chin. He was so high his entire body felt numb and breezy. The last thing he wanted to do was to get into a debate over whether his little brother was a head bussah or not. "Yo', I ain't mean it like that. All I'm saying is that I wouldn't have put you li'l niggas in that kind of danger. So, it's good, Kid gon' snatch what I'm sending, then load the trunk back up. As soon as he done y'all roll back to the Apple, it's as easy as fucking a drunk, bitch."

Bonkers laughed. "Yo, the God don' had his share of them kind, word up."

Kammron was trying his best not to feel so offended. He didn't like how Jimmy referred to them as li'l niggas, or how he seemed to talk down to them. He was accustomed to him doing such, but there was something about the moment that was irritating him.

"Yo', when we supposed to be doing this shit?"

Jimmy didn't like the way his words cut. He was a man of respect. He felt that every man shoulda approached and spoke to him in such a way. "Calm down, Killa. You, niggas, enjoy the party tonight and look forward to being on the road in two days. Let me get some shit in order, I'll be in touch."

Bonkers stood up and ran his hand over his face. He staggered a bit on his feet and caught his balance. "Dunn, you was making it seem like we was finna get that cream tonight. For my hopes all high and shit, but it's good. Fuck wit' a nigga when you get right. Until then, me and Kid finna see what this party do. Nah, mean?"

Jimmy gave him a half hug and a pat on his back. "No doubt, God." He wide stepped and got ready to give Kammron a half a hug but he stepped out of the back room, and into the party again.

That made Jimmy feel some type of way. When it came to his feelings for Kammron they ran hot and cold. One minute he was cool wit' the teen, the next he wanted to twist him. He ran his tongue across his teeth and slammed the door back.

Kammron grooved his way through the party, as Cardi B's track blasted out of the system. The females were twerking harder than ever it seemed. Their skirts were around their waists and their asses jiggled. It looked so good to them.

Bonkers threw his arms up, as a thick dark-skinned sister stopped in front of him, and turned her ass around, popping in his lap. "Word to my muthafuckin' mother!" he exclaimed, grinding with her.

Kammron held up the bottle of Ace of Spades. "This Harlem, son. This how we living in Harlem, Kid." He pulled a light-skinned, thick broad in front of him, and clutched her fat ass cheeks that were encased inside of a pair of coochie cutters. She moaned into his neck and pressed forward into his hard penis.

Bonkers watched it happen in slow motion. It was like he was having an out-of-body experience. The Puerto Rican female from earlier pointed at him, then Kammron from across the room. Then there was a short, heavyset, Spanish nigga with curly hair forcing his way through the crowd. When he got on the side of Kammron, he raised the Tequila bottle and smashed it on the side of Kammron's head. Kammron jerked forward and dropped to one knee.

Bonkers was like a bull rushing through the crowd. He picked the Puerto Rican high into the air, and threw him into the China cabinet, shattering the glass covering, and the dishes that were inside. Then he was on top of him hitting him with fist after fist, all face shots.

The Puerto Rican woman from earlier screamed at the top of her lungs. *"Stop-stop—get off him!"*

Kammron felt the blood drip from the cut in his head down to his neck. He made it to his feet and staggered in the direction of Bonkers. Before he could make it to him, he turned and slapped the Puerto Rican girl with all his might, knocking her out cold.

The crowd circled around Bonkers as he pummeled the man with big fists. By the time Kammron got to his side, he was standing up and looking down at the mess of the man he'd made.

"Yo', let's get the fuck out of here, God. That chump ain't getting up no time soon."

Chapter 3

Two days later, Kammron sat on the couch inside of Shelly's mother, Stacie's living room getting ready to roll a blunt. He was just finishing splitting it down the middle with his nail when Shana came from the back of the house rocking a pair of boy shorts that were up in her kitty. Her tight-white, wife-beater showcased her B cup breasts. She was braless, both nipples were visible through the material. Shana was Shelly's little sister.

"Dang, I hope you finna let me smoke wit' you?" she asked coming over, sitting next to him.

Kammron looked her over. The lamplight from the living room glistened off her thick golden thighs. She crossed them, and the material of her panties disappeared.

"Yo', get ya li'l ass up and go put some clothes on. If ya sister come home and catch you sitting around me like this she gon' whoop yo' li'l young ass."

Shana smacked her lips. "Please, ain't nobody worried about, Shelly. She ain't gon do shit to me, I'm grown. Besides, it's a free country, and this is my mama house. I can walk around this boy however I want, too. I can't help if my body makes you nervous." She stood up and turned around so that he could see her panties stuck up in her booty. She popped back on her legs. Shana was nice and thick, five-feet-four-inches tall. A hundred and thirty pounds and all-black, unlike her mixed sister Shelly.

Kammron eyed that ass and felt his dick getting hard. "Shorty what time yo' sister get home from work? I forgot."

Shana eased into his lap and situated herself. Her juicy cheeks found his pipe and trapped it. She leaned all the way back and rested her cheek against his. "She working a double trying to make manager. She ain't finna be back for at last another three hours." She took Kammron's right hand and slid it between her thighs.

His fingers played over the laced material. He could feel the heat from her middle resonate to his finger. She pulled the material aside and allowed him to lock his eyes on her bald lips. "Damn, Shana."

"What?" she whispered, opening her thighs wider. "Touch me, Kamm, please. I want you to touch me like you did before." Now her thighs were splayed widely.

Kammron forgot all about the blunt. His conscious was no longer a factor. All that mattered was the pussy that was before him. He rubbed the lips and licked his fingers. Then played over them again and added more saliva to his digits. He opened her labia wide and trailed circles around her clitoris.

She hopped in his lap. "Unhhh-shit, Kamm!" She threw her head back and began moaning at the top of her lungs. Her toes curled and her pussy got wetter and wetter.

Kammron felt a second of guilt, as he slid his index finger into her box. Her hole was barely able to accept it, he pulled it out and sucked it into his mouth. "Shorty, you gon' make me hit this ass. I'm telling you, you ain't ready for that shit yet."

She humped forward into his hand. "Yes, I am, please! Please, Killa—please test me. I want you to fuck me, right now!" She moaned and kissed his neck.

He nudged her away with his head. "Yo quit all that kissing shit. I save them lovey dovies for ya sister." He rubbed her lips and played with her wet slit. Her essence oozed out of her and pooled into his lap.

"Please fuck me, Kamm. I swear I won't tell nobody. On my mother, I'll keep this shit between me and you until the death of me." She stood up her bald pussy was smushed in between her thick thighs. It looked so good all wet and glistening to him.

He rubbed his hand over her ass cheeks and brought her forward, then kissed her peach. "Damn, this lil mafucka so juicy. I don't know how it fits between ya legs like this." He growled, opened the lips all the way up, and ran his tongue in circles around her button. She shook in his grasp. "Unnhhh-Killa-uhhh-Daddy! It feels so good. Please just fuck me, I'm ready—I swear I am." She stuck two fingers into herself and winced. Then placed her foot on the pillow of the couch, while he licked all over her fingers, and sucked her lips one by one.

Kamm flicked away at her bud, smacked her hand out of the way, and slipped two of his own fingers into her slot. He ran them in and out. The fit was tight. Slowly and after some work, he was able to push them deeper and deeper. Then he had them all the way inside of her. Her pussy felt like hot marshmallows.

Shana groaned and opened her thighs wider. "Yes-yes-uhhh—I'm cumming-I'm cumming." She shook and fell against him.

He pushed her over the arm of the couch and kneeled down between her legs from the back. He licked up and down her crease. Opened her ass cheeks and sucked her pussy from the back. The noises were loud and boisterous.

"Uhhhh-Kamm-unhhh-unnhhhh! Fuck me please-fuck me—I'm begging you!"

He slapped her ass. "Shut up!" He applied more licking and sucking on her clitoris. Her juices ran down her thick thighs. "Told you, you ain't ready yet, shorty." He added two fingers into her hole again and worked them at full speed while he sucked on her clit.

Shana threw her head back and hollered, "Unnhhhh-you're—too much-Killa—unhhh, you're-too-much. Fuck—I'm cumming-I'm cumming!"

He stood up, dropped his pants, and rubbed his dick up and down her slit while she spasmed in front of him. It took every ounce of willpower inside of him to not slip into that cat. Her pussy felt like it was beating—yearning for him. He pressed the head to her opening and was just about to ease the head inside when Stacie pulled in front of the house in her loud ass Station Wagon. Kammron jumped back and pulled his pants up.

Shana worked her boy shorts up her thighs and rushed down the hallway. She ran into her room and closed the door locking it with a butter knife. She hopped on the bed and finished off the nut that Kammron caused to mount inside of her womb.

Kammron jogged to the backdoor and broke out of the house. His dick was still throbbing in his pants, and the scent of Shana on his top lip drove him nearly insane.

****

Later that day, Bonkers pulled up in front of Stacie's crib rolling a black Buick Century with rust spots all over the door. He honked the horn three times and sat back in his seat. He'd tooted two lines of Tar and was feeling breezy. He had two .40 Glocks on his hip and a bulletproof vest across his chest. There was another one laying on the passenger seat reserved for Kammron.

Kammron came down the steps of the stoop with a frown on his face. He opened the door to the Buick, and it seemed to holler that it was junk as the metal bent inward before he could get the door all the way open. He picked up the bulletproof vest from the passenger seat and sat down. "Yo', Shelly getting on my nerves, Kid. I gotta get some scratch so I can get the fuck out of her mom's crib. Word up, and I almost fucked Shana li'l ass again."

Bonkers got too excited at that revelation. "No shit! Yo', what the fuck happened this time?" he asked pulling away from the curb. "Make sure you toss that Kevlar on, Dunn. If Harlem taught us one thing it's that we can't trust no muthafuckin' body. Ex what that nigga, Jimmy, spitting."

Kammron threw his black T-shirt over his head, and sat it in his lap, while he put on the Kevlar. "Yo', so the God was in the living room chilling when shorty stepped in that bitch wit' these li'l lace joints on. Them shits was all up in her creases and everything, Dunn. Word up, I'm talking I could see her camel toe clear as day. Long story short, I wound up eating that thang, fingering her, and rubbing my joint all up and down her slit until her, moms popped up. My word had Stacie been five minutes later, I woulda popped shorty li'l cherry, and buss that ass all the way in. I know she got some good-good, Kid." He threw his shirt over the vest.

Bonkers imagined how Shana looked the last time he'd seen her in a pair of Capri's that were so tight he could make out her panty line in the back. Her ass was nice and rounded, she was a true thick Harlem goddess. "Kid, no bullshit, I would've been fucked. You don' already ate the pussy. Fingered the pussy and rubbed ya mans all over it. The only thing you ain't did was fuck. If you trying to save face for Shelly, Son that ship has sailed."

Kammron threw his seatbelt across his chest. "Yo' what you mean by that?"

It began to drizzle outside, Bonkers turned on the windshield wipers and got on to the Interstate. "Nigga, I'm saying if you trying to do right by, Shelly, by not fuckin' her sister,

Kid you might as well cause if she ever finds out you did all of that she gon' be just as mad. So, why not fuck? I woulda been hit her thick ass."

"Yeah, well, I haven't yet and don't think them twinges of guilt don't be traveling through me like blood in my veins cause it do. I just ain't got that much of a conscious in my dick. I mean what nigga do?" Kammron asked, really wanting to know the answer to that question.

Bonkers shrugged his shoulders. "Yo', I don't know, Boss. It's too much pussy in the world for me to park my car into one garage and never pull into another. Besides these hoes ain't loyal."

"My word, Kid, you can say that shit again." Kammron took the blunt out of the ashtray and sparked it. "Yo', why Jimmy always doing bidness wit' these fuck niggas out here in, Jersey? What's so good about these clowns? I thought they were shiesty?"

Bonkers kept rolling. "New York niggas are the shiestiest. And Harlem runs New York so it ain't nothing we ain't used too. We gon' drop this shit off, and pick up whatever, bruh already got in motion, and go from there. I need that five stacks. That's breathing room before we come up on something else. Ya' feel me?"

"And you know I do, as only the God can." Kammron inhaled the smoke and cracked his window just a tad. "These mafuckas better be on some up and up shit, though. Anytime we step outside of the Apple, I just get a crazy feeling, Dunn. Ain't no place like New York."

"Nigga you right about that. Let's fuck wit' this new *Meek Mill* while we roll the interstate, God. Word up!" He turned up the outdated radio and allowed the music to beat out of the speakers.

****

Bonkers backed the Buick Century into the garage as the older Cuban man directed him. There were two bodyguards standing on each side of the door. They held fully automatic assault rifles in their hands. Their hair was silky and pulled back into ponytails. These bandits hailed directly from the island of Cuba.

The car continued to move back into the garage that looked as if it was used as an auto repair shop. There were tools along the walls, and it smelled like oil and gasoline.

"Yo, this shit got the li'l hairs on my arm standing up, bruh. I hate rolling into these eerie ass places that we don't know shit about," Kammron relayed, looking around in a paranoid state. He was wishing he hadn't blown the Loud. The Percocets weren't helping his case either.

"Fuck these niggas, God. If worst comes to worst, we in this shit together. These mafuckas will have to empty all them clips, Kamm, word up."

As soon as the car couldn't be backed up any further, Bonkers threw the car in park. He rolled down the window. "Yo', Jimmy, say the shit in the trunk. Y'all pop that bitch and give us what we got coming," Bonkers hollered.

Diego stepped to the driver's window and tried the door handle. "Get out, I need to see who I'm conducting business with. Make sure you're not a rat."

Bonkers scrunched his face. "I ain't no muthafuckin' rat, son. Do I look like I crawl along the curb of the sidewalk, huh?"

Diego snapped his fingers the two bodyguards rushed over to the Buick and pointed their guns at both Kammron and Bonkers. "Get the fuck out of the car, both of you," Diego advised, calmly.

T.J. Edwards

Kammron clenched his jaw. "Yo', what the fuck you wanna do Bonkers" We can clap these niggas, B. My word I ain't going out like no pussy. That shit ain't in my blood, Kid."

Bonkers eyed Diego closely. "Nah, son, maybe this just the procedure. Let's gon' get out of the whip. We can always make these mafuckas pay for pulling these gats on us later." Bonkers grabbed the door handle and banged his shoulder against it. The door squeaked open and he stepped out with a mug on his face.

Kammron took another second and cursed under his breath. He didn't like niggas pulling guns in him if they weren't prepared to use them. He was from the old school, thought of Harlem that said if you up it and don't use it then you owe your enemy your life on their terms.

"Pussy muthafuckas." He opened the car door and stood up. "Yo', take them gats off of us, niggas. We did what the old head said."

Diego told them to lower their weapons in Spanish. He extended his hand to Bonkers. "I don't mean any disrespect. You're taught as a young boy in, Havana, that a man must be able to look another man in the eyes before, and while he is conducting business with him."

Bonkers mugged his hand and refused to shake it. "Yo', ma nigga, and in Harlem if you pull a gun on a nigga you better be ready to use it or be ready to lose your life because you didn't."

Kammron watched all three men closely. He kept his hand at the ready. He could already feel the Glock in his hand as it bussed. He hated the Spanish men for aiming their guns at them. No matter how well the mission went he could never forget what they'd done.

Bonkers grabbed the keys out of the steering wheel, then headed to the back of the car. He placed the key inside of it and opened the trunk. There were two Batman book bags inside of it. "Yo', my brother sent this. You supposed to have something for me too, though."

Diego looked at his hand and smiled. He felt disrespected, he'd extended his hand in a formal greeting, and Bonkers had rejected him. He glared at the young man and felt like spitting in his face. Instead, he grunted and stepped beside Bonkers. Then pulled one of the book bags from the back of the trunk and peeked inside after unzipping it.

T.J. Edwards

Chapter 4

Diego rummaged through the book bag, then brought it to the front of the car and slammed it on the hood. "What the fuck is this?" he asked seeing that there were the usual five bricks of Tar inside of it.

For as long as he'd been doing business with Jimmy, he'd always sent him ten bricks, five in each book bag. He was sure this time would be no different, but since Bonkers had neglected to show him respect by not shaking his hand he was looking for a way to make, he and Kammron pay for the disrespect. He stormed to the back of the car and grabbed the other book bag out of the trunk.

He checked inside it and saw that it also contained five bricks, as was per his and Jimmy's agreement. "This one is short, too."

Bonkers frowned and felt uneasy. "Yo', what the fuck you talking about, Dunn?"

Diego sneered at him, he stepped up to a big toolbox and pulled out a book bag containing one-hundred and fifty thousand dollars. "You two sons of bitches come all the way from New York to short change me, huh? You motherfuckers think I'm an idiot—do you?"

Kammron lowered his eyes. "Fuck is you talking about, nigga, we ain't did shit. We got word that you was supposed to grab those bags out of the trunk and send us back wit' something. You got yo' shit, now give us what we got coming, Kid."

"Word up, mafuckas gotta be on they way back to the Big Apple before the Interstate get infested with Troopers and shit," Bonkers said, feeling his blood boil.

Diego turned his back to them. The light from the garage shined down on the bald spot in the back of his head. "Did he tell you what you were bringing me?"

"Yo', that ain't our bidness. We gave you what he sent, now drop our shit off, son. We gotta be on our way." Bonkers clenched and unclenched his fists.

Diego tightened his grip on the book bags. "You tell, Jimmy, he can't play me, and to kiss my ass. He's just like his no-good father, Ruiz. Both of them are nothing more than scavengers. You two get the fuck out of New Jersey or lose your lives." He reached inside of his suit coat.

For Kammron all bets were off. As soon as he saw the old head reach inside of his coat, he threw caution to the wind. He came up with both Glock .40s and started dumping at his security taking them by surprise.

Boom! Boom! Boom! Boom! Boom!

The guns roared like angry Lions before a kill. The first two slugs caught one of Diego's bodyguards in the side of the head and knocked half of his face off. The third and fourth bullet slammed into the back wall of the shop, and the fifth bullet caught the second bodyguard in the forehead. It punched his brain out the back of his head and sent little pieces of his noodles baking on the floor. Blood gushed out of his opening and poured onto the concrete.

Diego cursed in Spanish and took off running. He pulled out his cellphone and began hollering into it that Jimmy had set him up. That Jimmy sent assassins at him. Bonkers was on his ass with his Glock. He stopped mid-stride, aimed his Glock and fired.

Boom!

The bullet traveled at the speed of sound, and slammed into Diego's back, twisting the man around. Bonkers ran up to him and placed the gun to his forehead.

36

Coke Kings

"Harlem here, son."

Boom! Boom! Pieces of Diego's brain went flying in every direction.

He was dead before he hit the ground. Bonkers stood over him and remembered how he felt when the Spanish men aimed their guns at him. Since Diego was their head, he took it most personally with him. He aimed his gun and pulled the trigger three more times splattering his face.

Kammron ran up beside him and looked down at the fallen Cuban. "Pussy ass, nigga. He kicked him in the ribs three times. Yo', if you up yo' gun and don't use it, you forfeit your life to your enemy on their terms. That's the way the game go. Yo', let's get back to Harlem, Kid, fuck Jersey."

****

Three hours later, Kammron sat in Jimmy's living room while he paced back and forth with his shirt off. Kammron was eating on a double cheeseburger, and a large order of French Fries, across from him Bonkers was smashing a Gyro with extra meat, and cucumber sauce. Both men were smacking loud. For some reason murder always made them hungry. Jimmy shook his head so hard he felt a migraine coming on. He couldn't believe what they'd told him. The last people he wanted to be beefing with was Diego's River Boys.

"Yo', Kid, I told you niggas to do one fuckin' thing. You, niggas, had one task, and y'all couldn't even do that. Now I gotta watch out for these Old-World Cubans because of you, niggas' fuck up. Son, this shit ain't right."

Bonkers sucked his fingers, he had a mouth full of Gyro. "Yo, nigga you weren't there. You ain't see how them Cubans was about to dead us." Bonkers stopped to chew some more of his food. "If we hadn't handled our business them." He

37

stopped and chewed some more, closed his eyes, and smiled. "Damn this good," he said after he swallowed.

Kammron busted up laughing, as he took another huge bite of his Double cheeseburger. He was high as a hot air balloon in the sky.

"Yo' this shit ain't funny, B. I'm finna have to go to war over this shit. Y'all murked, Diego. That was the second oldest son in the River Boys Posse from back home in Cuba. Them fools are dangerous, not to mention that could slow down my flow coming from the Island. I ain't trying to see them jokers like that, B. They take that savage shit to a whole new level. New York ain't got shit on Havana."

Kammron felt offended. "Nigga fuck Havana, we from Harlem, Boss. The world begins and ends in Harlem. Them Havana niggas can't do shit to us that we can't do to them. That's word to, Kathy, right there."

"Yeah, Jimmy, you making it seem like they stopped making guns in New York. We just proved that they can't fuck wit' our bidness, Dunn. They want that beef shit we'll spot they ass up like cows then," Bonkers snapped then took a huge bite from his Gyro.

Jimmy lowered his head. He was frustrated because he saw that Bonkers and Kammron didn't understand how the game went. There was just certain Posses that you didn't get into it with. Certain players that you had to respect and the River Boys was a crew that he had to respect and stay in good graces with so that it kept things on a cordial level back in Havana. He knew it was only a matter of time before word got back to the Island, and a war broke out in the states. That could cost him hundreds of thousands of dollars. Hundreds of thousands that he couldn't afford to lose.

Bonkers stood up and wiped his mouth with a napkin. "Say, Jimmy, why don't you just have us go and knock off the rest of those fools then? If you're so worried about them clapping back. Shid, me and the homie ain't got no problem cleaning up our mess. Ain't that right, Kamm?"

Kammron stuffed three French fries into his mouth and continued to chew a jaw full of double cheeseburger. He spoke with his mouth full of food. "None whatsoever." He spit and closed his eyes to finish chewing. He slipped the straw past his lips and drank a nice portion of the Pepsi.

Bonkers busted out laughing again. "Yo', Kid eating like he starving. That shit funny as hell." He fell on the couch holding his stomach.

Then Kammron was cracking up, and still trying to chew his food. "Shut up, Bonkers shut yo' ass up." They got to laughing so hard that they couldn't stop.

Jimmy was fuming. "Both of you li'l niggas, shut the fuck up!" he snapped. "Y'all honestly don't realize how fucked up this shit really is. But you muthafuckas will when bodies start dropping all around, New York. Damn, I don't need this shit! Something told me not to send you li'l niggas."

Kammron sat on the couch clenching his jaw. His fists were balled tight. "Yo, not once have you said you appreciate us for handling this bidness for you. Not once have you apologized for sending us into that danger zone. That fool said you ain't send enough work. He said you wasn't shit just like your father, Ruiz and that you could kiss his ass."

"Then he reached in his coat and got ready to pull out a gat to clap us, and the homie reacted. Had he not, me—*your li'l brother* woulda been dead as a muthafucka. So, get the fuck off your high horse, and thank by man's for saving mine, and his life." Bonkers stepped to him.

Jimmy looked into his eyes and flared his nostrils. "Bonkers, if you don't sit yo' li'l ass down we about to tear this mafucka up. Nigga, I don't give a fuck how tough you think you is, I'm still your big brother. Sit yo' ass down!"

Bonkers mugged him. "Apologize for sending us off, Jimmy."

"What?" Jimmy scoffed. "Nigga sit yo' ass down."

Kammron slid his hand under his shirt. He didn't know where things were headed, but if he had to, he would clap Jimmy over Bonkers in a heartbeat. "Y'all chill, Gods, it ain't a big deal."

"N'all fuck that, B. He supposed to be my oldest brother, and this nigga almost got my life took. This nigga gon' apologize to me and you, or he's right we finna fuck this living room up. Ain't no bitches over here, son. Apologize, or let's turn the fuck up." He stepped forward again until their noses were touching.

Kammron's hand was clutching the gun now. His finger was on the trigger. If he pulled it out, he was sure he was going to start bussing. He didn't give two fucks about, Jimmy never had. There was only room in his heart to love one dude, and that dude was Bonkers. "Son, I'm warning both of you niggas to chill. Bonkers you already know how I am."

Bonkers shook his head. "Fuck that, Kid, we put our lives in the line and this nigga ain't even so much as offered to buss down that bread wit' us. The bread, or the dope. He thinks we still some li'l ass kids a something. Mafucka gon' respect me, and you. Nigga apologize or I'm stealing you."

Jimmy pulled his hair back into a ponytail. "Ain't no nigga gon' make me do shit. Y'all ain't got a clue of what I'm about to go through because of the shit y'all did—"

Bonkers reached back and swung as hard as he could. *Bam!* His knuckles slammed into Jimmy's jaw and staggered him. Jimmy fell backward and held himself up by use of the wall.

"Fool ass, nigga, fuck Havana. This Harlem, all you do is talk about that punk ass island. Harlem is black heaven, nigga. Respect this turf and respect us."

Jimmy felt the blood dripping from his lip. He dabbed his fingers on it and looked his digits over. "You muthafucka, you bussed me in my shit."

"You, betta believe it. Apologize, nigga, apologize right the fuck now." Bonkers pulled his shirt over his head. He kept the vest in place though.

Jimmy nodded. "Let's take this shit to the basement. You wanna put yo' fuckin' hands on me. Let's go down here and get it."

"Nigga you ain't said nothing but a word, and when I'm done you gon' give us half of them bricks, and half of the money dude was finna pay you. Let's go," Bonkers ordered taking off toward the back of the house.

When they got downstairs, Bonkers unsnapped his Kevlar vest and tossed it to Kammron. He jumped up and down and rolled his head around on his shoulders. "Yo', I'm ready, nigga."

Jimmy cracked his knuckles and balled his fists. He held them at chin level. "Bring the noise li'l, nigga."

Kammron stood back with a mug on his face. He was praying that Bonkers didn't wind up losing in the fight. He didn't give a fuck who Jimmy was to him if his homeboy started to lose, he was jumping in. They had never been able to sit around and watch each other box one on one before. It may have started out that way in the past, but it always ended with the both of them getting in their enemy's ass together.

"Y'all hurry up and get this suit over wit' so we can buss down that merch."

Jimmy glared at him. "Ain't shit to buss down. Everything in then bags belongs to me. I'm finna whoop his li'l ass, and—"

Bam! Bam! Bam!

Bonkers hit him with a three-punch combo. Two to the jaw, and a jab straight to the nose busting his shit.

"You talk too much."

Jimmy flew into the brick wall and bounced back up. "You muthafucka! You want some of me, huh?" He came swinging haymakers.

Bonkers lowered his head into his guards. He blocked two of his blows and got caught by the third and fourth ones. His lips were busted, and his jaw pained him. But the feeling of being in a fight excited him to his very core. He rushed Jimmy at full speed throwing punches. Right and left hooks, each blow rattling Jimmy, and knocking him backward. He wrapped his arms around his body and flipped him on his back. He was just about to straddle him when Jimmy kneed him in the nuts. It hurt so bad that Bonkers fell off him and on to his side curled into a ball. Jimmy eased up and wiped the blood from his nose. He took a step back, then jumped forward and kicked Bonkers as hard as he could in the ribs. So hard it flipped him on to his stomach.

"You, bitch ass li'l nigga, I run this shit. You thought it was sweet, get yo li'l punk ass up."

Kammron swung, and punched Jimmy on the side of the jaw, knocking him out cold. Jimmy seemed to fall in slow motion. He landed on his side, his face ricocheted off the concrete.

"Watch yo' muthafuckin' mouth, nigga. That's my brother, Dunn. You don't put yo' muthafuckin' feet on him." He cocked back and kicked him as hard as he could in the ribs. Then straddled him getting ready to pound him out.

Coke Kings

"Wait!" Bonkers eased up, his balls were killing him. He staggered with his left hand between his legs cupping his nuts. He was nearly out of breath. He felt like he was seconds away from throwing up. "Chill out, Kid, don't fuck him up. He didn't know better, B," he winced and exhaled slowly. "We just gon' take what's ours and leave that nigga wit' the rest. Let the cards fall where they may."

Kammron looked into Jimmy's red face. Jimmy was just coming back to consciousness. "Yo', if this a been anybody else I'da beat 'em senseless. This nigga lucky he yo' brother." He got up and stood beside Bonkers. "Let's get our scratch and get the fuck up out of here."

Bonkers looked down on his brother. "Get ya ass up, and give us what we deserve."

T.J. Edwards

Chapter 5

Kammron stepped to his mother Kathy's door and knocked on it. He held the bouquet of white roses behind his back and smiled. He knew she had to be peeking through the peephole. He still hated the fact that she had to live in the Harlem River Houses which were nothing more than a Project building. One of his goals was to move her away from those slums that she loved so much. He wanted to buy her an estate somewhere out in Manhattan, or Staten Island.

Kathy ran her fingers through her unkempt hair. She wiped her mouth and tried her best to put on a brave front. She unlocked the door and pulled it open. "Hey, baby! What brings you over here?"

Kammron's heart sank at the sight of his mother. She wore a long white T-shirt that was covered in Kool-Aid stains. Her hair was a mess. She smelled funky, and he caught an even worst whiff coming out of her apartment. He felt like a straight loser. He handed her the roses.

"Yo, these are for you gorgeous." He pulled her into his embrace and kissed her cheek.

Kathy looked over the roses and blushed. "Damn, Kamm, you always doing shit like this. I don't deserve no got damn roses." She sniffed them and smiled. "Come on in." She waved for him to follow her inside.

He reluctantly stepped inside. Everywhere he looked there seemed to be crawling cockroaches. The house though sparsely furnished looked a mess. The floor had crumbs all over it. The garbage can was full of trash. The table had two plates with food contents still stuck to it. The sink was full of dishes. He saw more than one rat run across the kitchen floor, and the couch looked filthy. It made him uncomfortable to even be there. He got ready to close the door when a dope head from down the hall caught it.

"Wait-wait-wait, I need to ask Kathy a question!" she yelled with her short Afro all nappy, and full of lint. She wore a bright red jogging suit that looked three sizes too big.

Kamm backed up and looked toward Kathy. "Yo moms, you know this bitch?"

Kathy nodded. "Yeah, that's my girl from down the hall. What you want, Dee?" Kathy asked, looking past him.

"Girl, I need to borrow a syringe. Jack done took my last one, and I just got a blessing from my nephew on the first floor. I'll share if you hook me up."

"Bitch don't bring ya funky ass back down to my mom's shit no more. Word is bond if I catch you and her together again, I'ma put three coppers in ya forehead." Kammron slammed the door in her face.

Dee ran away from the door in sheer terror. "Okay-okay!" she hollered over her shoulder.

Kammron made up the distance between him and Kathy with three strides. He snatched her up and held her to the wall. "Yo', you back to shooting that shit in ya veins ma, huh?"

"Let me down, Kammron—let me go, right now!" she ordered trying to twist out of his grasp.

He held her firmer. "Answer my question. Are you back on that needle?" The stench of her hurt his stomach. It made him feel sicker than a child with the flu.

"Let me go, Kamm! You ain't my daddy. I'm ya muthafuckin' mother—this is my house." She beat at his hands again.

He released her and watched her fall to the floor. The sight of her in that state brought his depression on full fledge. He began to worry and felt weak and worthless. "Yo', I thought you beat that shit, ma. Since when you went back to using?"

Kathy got to her feet and dusted the dead cock Roach off of her knees. Her mouth was dry. The remnants of her high were wearing away quickly. She scratched her inner forearm, right at the injection site. "Boy, I ain't lasted two weeks sober. How can I? That shit be calling me like a stalker in the middle of the night." She closed her eyes and squeezed tears down her cheeks. She wasn't really sad but knew that Kammron tended to take it easier on her if he saw her in tears.

Kammron looked off and took a deep breath. "Moms whenever I see you like this, I get to doing this kind of shit." He reached into the small of his back and pulled out a .357 Magnum. There was already one bullet in the chamber. He opened the cylinder and spun it. Clicked it back in place, and held the barrel to his temple, after pulling back the hammer.

Kathy backed away from him. "Kamm, what are you doing, baby? What are you about to do wit' that thing?" She was terrified.

Kammron frowned and squeezed the trigger. It clicked loudly, he squeezed it again. *Click!* Then took it away from his temple. "Yo, I can't take seeing you like this. It makes me sick to my stomach." He popped the cylinder out again and spun it. Placed the gun back to his temple and pulled the trigger twice.

Each time he squeezed the trigger Kathy jumped. She imagined what it would look like if he killed himself in front of her. Ever since Kammron was a little kid she'd known him to become deeply depressed, and suicidal. Though he didn't start making attempts on his life until he was in his teens. She'd caught him trying to hang himself at fourteen, and at fifteen he took a bunch of pills. He'd been diagnosed with severe depression and bipolar disorder. As he got older, he learned how to manage his episodes by use of drugs, and alcohol. He abruptly moved out of her home at the age of sixteen and had been on his own ever since.

Kathy walked toward him and reached for the gun. "Baby, I'm sorry, Mama is trying to get better, but you doing shit like this ain't gon' help me either. Have you been taking your medication?"

Kammron waved her off. "Them white folks ain't finna poison me. I ain't taking that shit, I don't need it. You the reason, I am how I am." He spun the cylinder and placed it back to his temple. He pulled the trigger three quick times. *Click! Click! Click!* Kammron began to pace back and forth. "Yo', I came over here to take you shopping, and to pay all of your bills. But when I come, I find you living in this filth. Trading needles and shit wit' yo' junkie neighbors." He spun the cylinder, placed the gun in his mouth and pulled the trigger four quick times. *Click! Click! Click! Click!* Tears ran down his eyes, he loved his mother so much.

Kathy kneeled to her knees. "Please baby, stop it—please! I can't take the agony of wondering if that gun is going to go off or not. I can't live without you, Son. I'm just struggling, right now. Mama is really going through it." She covered her face and sobbed into her hands.

Kammron's heart became heavy. He lowered the gun and sighed. "Mama chill, stop crying please."

Kathy continued to break down, she felt horrible, she felt weak-less than a woman. How could she have allowed herself to stoop so low? How could she have given a man all of her power? So much so that she lost herself in the process? After Kammron's father finished dragging her through the mud she needed a way out. Needed a safe haven, so she turned to the arms of the drugs that he'd led her on to. Heroin became her refuge, her safe place-her heaven on earth. Within the drug, she was able to find unconditional love, and contentment.

She scooted down to her backside and wrapped her arms around her knees. "I'm sorry, baby, I'm so-so sorry!"

Kammron snapped out of his zone, and squatted down on the floor next to her, before sitting on his butt. He pulled her into his embrace and kissed her forehead. "I love you, Goddess. I know you going through a lot but real soon, I'ma take you away from all of this garbage down here. Son know you just trying to find a way to escape the madness. A way to battle against the pain that my father took you through, and left you in. Yo', I get it, and I'm sorry for coming down on you like that my Queen. You hear me?"

Kathy sniffed snot back into her nose. "I'm nobody's, Queen, baby. I'm just a broken woman with no direction, and no soul. I feel more lost than a kid's mitten at recess." She swallowed the lump in her throat and cried into his neck.

Kammron rubbed her back. "Yo' I got you, I'ma pay a few housekeepers to come down here and get your spot in order. Then we finna go out to get something to eat, and I'ma take you shopping. You still the God's Queen no matter how you're feeling, right now." He kissed her again, then pulled her to her feet.

She ran her fingers through her hair. "Boy, are you out of your mind? I can't go nowhere looking like this." She felt so ugly, she dared not look into her mirror, she already knew what she was in for.

"Later for that jazz you talking. I just got one hell of a payday, and I want my moms to spend a night out on the town wit' me. All expenses paid of course. Oh, and before we even get into all of that, I ain't asking you, I'm telling you that we finna go. So, chop chop, boogie boogie."

Kathy stared at him for thirty full seconds. "You're always trying to make sure that everybody else is well taken care of. But what about yourself, son, huh? What's really going on inside of you?" She stepped in front of him and rested her hands on his chest.

Kammron took her left one and kissed the back of it. "Long as my mother is taken care of don't nothing else matter to me. You already know what it is."

Kathy shook her head. "Look, you can leave that tough talk fo them hooligans out there in Harlem. You're talking to your mother, right here. I know you, I want to know how my son is really doing? What's going on inside of your heart baby? Please tell me, I need to know?"

Kammron kissed her forehead and pulled out a wad of hundreds. He counted off ten of them and handed it to her. "Look this q gee right here. You can get anything that you wanna get wit' it. I just want you to enjoy yourself, the only stipulation is that you go out on the town wit' me tonight. That a deal?"

Kathy already had the thousand dollars spent. She was imagining a table full of heroin, and brand-new syringes, amongst other things. She was thinking she could even throw a party. The spending of the money in her brain boosted the serotonin in her brain, and she couldn't stop smiling.

"Baby, you know what, we can do whatever you wanna do. It's been a while since we painted the town red, so you know what, let's do it."

Kammron pulled her to him again and rested his lips against her forehead. His depression was trying its best to break him down to his lowest self, but with everything that he had inside of him, he was going to fight it until he had his head back straight. Spending time with his mother always seemed to put him back to where he needed to be.

"Remember moms, anything you want this night you can have. It's all about you, I mean that."

Coke Kings

Chapter 6

The doorbell rung for the fourth time, after the first Bonkers made his way down the hallway with a face towel in his hand he'd soaked in alcohol. He ran it over his face as he stepped to the door and peeked out of the hole.

"Shit." He rolled his eyes. "Yo' Yasmin, what's really good, shorty? I don't feel like fuckin' wit' you today."

Yasmin was a lil Dame that Bonkers had smashed one time back when he was thirteen years old. She'd disappeared to Virginia, and he hadn't seen her for five years. Suddenly she reappeared with a four-year-old little girl swearing up and down that she was his kid. Bonkers had been giving her the cold shoulder cause, he didn't believe her. Yasmin was a bit of a mystery to him and had quite the track record before her God-fearing parents caught wind of it and sent her to stay with her grandparents in Virginia.

Yasmin beat on the door. "Yo Bonkers, I can see ya black ass through the hole in the door. Open up and let's get an understanding about, my baby. Son, I can't do this shit on my own." She waited a few seconds and beat again. "Bonkers, what the deal, God?"

Bonkers lowered his head. "Yo,' check it, Yasmin, I ain't tryna go there wit' you today, Goddess. The God got a lot of shit on his plate already. I ain't tryna come up with no extras."

She banged in the door as hard as she could. "Open this mafuckin' door! Open this mafuckin' door! Open this mafuckin' door! *Open it-open it—open it!*"

Bunkers yanked the door open and grabbed her by her throat. He picked her up in the air and began to choke her as hard as he could, squeezing the life out of her. "Bitch, I told you about coming over here to the Projects fuckin' wit' a nigga didn't I, huh? Didn't I tell you to leave me the fuck alone about this baby shit?"

Yasmin closed her eyes and didn't make a sound. She wasn't about to give him the time of day. If he was going to kill her for asking for support of her daughter, then she would die in her kid's honor. There was no way she was about to allow Bonkers to be a dead beat. She'd been taking care of their daughter on her own since the baby had come into existence inside of her womb. It wasn't fair, she felt her air leaving her lungs, and became dizzy.

Bunkers squeezed harder and then dropped her to the floor. He slammed the door and stood over her. "Now what the fuck do you want, Yasmin?"

Yasmin grabbed her neck and struggled to breathe. She looked up at him and lowered her eyes. Then came to her feet, she looked him in the eyes for a long time. "You don't need to be putting your hands on me, Bonkers. I ain't never did nothing to you to make you treat me the way you been treating me."

Yasmin was five feet two inches tall. She weighed a hundred and twenty-five pounds. She was dark-skinned, with natural silky hair that was done up in shoulder length micro braids that her mother had done for her.

Bonkers walked into the kitchen and opened the refrigerator. He took out a bottle of Apple juice, came back and handed it to her. "Yo,' you been back for a month, and ever since you been back you been driving me nuts. I know, I ain't get you pregnant before you left. You was fucking all kinds of niggas, including, Kamm."

"See now that's a lie, I never screwed, Kammron. We fooled around, but he never put his stuff inside of me. The only boy that did that was you. But you ain't gotta take my word for it." She reached into her purse and came up with an invitation to attend the Maury show. She handed it to him.

Bonkers looked it over. "Yo, what the fuck is this?"

"You wanna find out if you're, Yazzy's father you ain't gotta pay shit. They gon fly you out to take a DNA test. Hell, if you think Kammron could be he father, I'll have them fly him out, too. I ain't worried because I know who my baby daddy is, and his ass is you." She stared at him. "So, what you wanna do?"

Bonkers laughed and handed the invitation back to her. "Yo', where is this li'l girl, right now?"

"Her name is Yazzy, and she's four years old. She is currently staying with my mother as well as myself. We in the Projects around the corner barely making ends meet."

Bonkers scoffed. "Yo', so is that what this is about, huh? It's about you looking for a muthafuckin' payday?"

Yasmin winced she was so frustrated, she felt like swinging off on Bonkers. She knew he woulda killed her, but she was starting to care less and less. "Look it ain't solely about the money."

"But it's about it somewhat, though?" He laughed and grabbed a juice out of the refrigerator.

"Hell, yeah its apart of the equation." She wanted to scream. She took a deep breath and tried her best to calm down. "Do you have any idea how hard it is to raise a kid alone these days? How much they cost, and how hard it is to get ahead once you have them? Bonkers, I'm drowning, right now and I need help—your help. She is your daughter, if you don't, believe me, you can take a DNA test, or you can take this trip to the Maury show. I'm game either way you wanna go. Oh, and well just look." She pulled out her Galaxy phone and showed him the pictures of Yazzy.

Bonkers looked the picture over and stared at it long and her in disbelief. Yazzy looked like a carbon copy of his mother when she was a little girl. Second to that she had his thick eyebrows and almond-shaped eyes. That blew his mind. He did all that he could to not show his astonishment. He handed her back the phone.

"I'm not seeing any resemblance, but it's good. Give me a day to think things over, and I'll let you know which way I wanna go. In the meantime, how much loot you sitting on, right now?"

She broke eye contact with him. "I'm broke, I'm still trying to find me a reliable job but it's hard out here. The cost of childcare is kicking my ass. I gotta argue with my mother every time I need her to watch my child, and most times she still says no. You know she got a drinking problem, so I don't be trusting her guardianship no damn way."

"Shorty, I don't know nothing about you or your mother. But it's good, here!" He counted out two gees. "I know this ain't much, but hopefully it'll float you along until we can come to an understanding."

Yasmin wanted to knock the money out of his hand and kick his ass. Instead, she snatched it and counted it out, before stuffing it into her bra. "Two thousand dollars can't make up for four years being absent as a father. You need to get on your game real fast, Bonkers. My baby needs you."

****

Kammron twisted his key into the lock and stepped inside of the apartment. When his eyes picked up on Yasmin a smirk came across his lips. She'd had one of the fattest coochies he'd ever seen when they were kids. If he closed his eyes, he could see it clear as day. "Yo', what's good wit shorty, B? What we about to buss her down?"

Yasmin frowned. "Ugh, hell n'all, I ain't no li'l naive girl no more. I'm a grown ass woman!"

Kammron smacked his lips. "Bitch, who you popping off at. My word I'll smack you in that mafucka you keep talking. That's on, Kathy." He closed the door and stepped over to her.

Yasmin knowing that Kammron was known for being a straight animal throughout the slums of Harlem, backed up to create space. She could smell the scent of death coming off him. "Kamm ain't nobody got a problem wit' you. I'm just letting you know that this ain't that type of party no more."

Kammron sucked his teeth. "I only fuck wit bad hoes now anyway. You was just practice pussy for a nigga back in the day."

Bonkers mugged her. "Bitch I thought you said he never fucked?"

"He didn't fuck." She turned to Kammron. "Nigga you never fucked me. When me and Bonkers got down that was my first time ever having actual intercourse." She felt so offended.

Kammron rubbed his chin. He was really trying to remember if he'd fucked her or not. "Yo', I specifically remember how ya pussy look. You got one of them real chubby joints. There is a mole right above your sex lips.

Bonkers frowned. "Yo', this bitch just stood here and told me a bald-faced lie. I'ma need you to get the fuck out of my shit, right now, Yasmin. Take that lil scratch and get lost."

"Wait, me and you ain't never went all the way Kammron. I swear on my baby we didn't. I can't believe you finna stand here and make him think that we did when we didn't."

56

"I can't remember if we did or not, but I know that pussy is familiar to me." Kammron laughed and headed to the bathroom.

Yasmin was frustrated. She walked toward the door and stopped directly in front of it. "Look, I swear I never screwed ya mans. Yazzy is yours, I'm not asking for much. All I'm asking is that you get into her life and that you help me with her. I can't do it on my own." She opened the door and stepped into the hallway. "Please, Bonkers, here's my cell number, Facebook, and Snapchat information. Get at me as soon as you can. She's dying to meet her father."

"Yo shorty stop saying that shit until we get confirmation. But I heard you out, and I'ma get at you real soon. That's my word, be safe out there." He closed the door.

Yasmin took a deep breath and gathered herself before walking out of the Projects, and down the street toward her mother's buildings. She felt so dirty. So alone. So aggravated.

Kammron came out of the bathroom with a smile on his face. "Kid, what the deal wit' shorty ass?"

Bonkers sat at the living room table and poured out a quarter gram of Tar. He separated it into four lines, took a hundred-dollar bill, rolling it up. "Bitch say she got my shorty. A lil girl, her name, Yazzy." He leaned, tooted a line hard and held his head back while the drug took its effect.

Kammron sat across from him. "Yo, I know you ain't about to fall for that okey-doke. Hoes been putting kids on niggas since the beginning of time. It's one of the oldest tricks in the book."

"Yeah, only this time I don't think it's a trick. That lil girl look just like me, Son. She looked like Janine more than anything, though. I don't know what to do but it's been fucking wit' my anxiety ever since I saw those pictures. I think I gotta stand up and handle my bidness."

Kammron was silent for a minute. "Yo, let me see the flicks."

Bonkers tooted another line hard and pinched his nostrils closed as the drip began to descend down the back of his throat. He swallowed the poisoned mucous. "She ain't leave 'em. They were on her phone, but trust the God, that's my seed, Dunn. That's fucked up ain't it?"

Kammron hopped up. "Hell, n'all it ain't. Matter fact we need to go snatch up lil shorty and blow a few gees on her. Where they living at?"

"River Houses, Shorty say they barely surviving. Son, she was ready to take me to Maury to prove to me that I'm her daughter's father. She even had an invitation. Said if I wanted to get you tested, she would have them send you a ticket too. I guess they'll pay for everything."

Kammron busted up laughed. "No, bull shit—Maury! Nigga I say we go on that Bitch and act a fool, what you say?"

Bonkers was high as the statue of Liberty's torch. "It's in Connecticut, I'm game if you are. We could use the trip."

"Not only that but I got this one Homie from Malcolm Shabazz that just moved out to Stanford. His brother supposedly came up on twenty bricks of that Vietnamese raw. We could buss that move and come back to the Apple and off them suckers. Unless you wanna get a few of the project kids to turn this building out. It's a whole bunch of them running around all dirty and shit.

"We could pay they ass every week wit' a lil bit a nothing to do the heavy lifting for us. You know how the game go. We could break all ten of them keys down into nickels. Snatch up some of that Vietnamese shit, and really go hard. I'm ready to hop out in the streets inside of a peanut butter and Jelly Jag. This Bitch I know got a plug out in Nebraska on retagged whips. I'm tryna cash in and see what's really good."

Bonkers nodded out and caught his head before it fell into his lap. His eyes opened just a tad. "Say, Kid all of that shit sound—" He nodded off again.

Kammron could hear him snoring. "Ain't this about a bitch?" he began.

"Real good to me, you make sure when you holler at that bitch for one of them whips that you tell her—" More snoring.

Kammron grabbed an Orange juice from the refrigerator, sipped from it, and walked back into the living room. He watched Bonkers scratch himself profusely. He slapped his hand on the table.

Bonkers eyes opened. "Tell her I said that I want one of them, bad boys, too. Ain't no way my right-hand gon be riding clean, and I'm rolling on the subway. You feel me, God?"

Kammron laid his head on the back of the couch. "Yeah, I feel you, Kid. Gon' sleep that shit off. I'ma get at you in a few hours." He closed his eyes as he felt his depression taking over him. He searched his waist for the .357 and began to panic once he saw that he'd left it at his mother's crib. "It's cool, I just gotta pull through this. I'll be alright, I'm stronger than this shit." He sat down the juice and dozed off with Bonkers.

Chapter 7

It had been two weeks since the fight with Jimmy. Now Bonkers was rolling the stolen Chevy Caravan to the curb so Jimmy could get inside.

"Yo', I still don't trust this nigga, Kid. I don't know no nigga from Harlem that's gon take an ass whoopin', then carry on like ain't nothing happened, unless they had some ill shit up their sleeve. I know Kid your brother in all, but son gotta be up to something." Kammron vented.

It was two o'clock in the morning, and they were set to buss a move with Jimmy that was supposed to be the first step in rectifying the River Boy's hit. Jimmy had been very stingy with the details. That was another reason why Kammron's paranoia and anxiety were going through the roof.

"Push, come to shove, nigga you my brother over any brother. I'd hate to twist my own blood but if I have too just know it's us against the world, Dunn. Word to Janine!"

"Word to Kathy, Kid," Kammron retorted.

Without saying so many words they understood each other.

Jimmy got into the truck with a Freddy Kruger mask already on his head. "Since you, niggas got paid half of the profits, I'ma about to show y'all what we gotta do to send a message to the underworld."

He slid the mask up on his face just a little so they could see his face. "Now listen, I told you niggas all of this shit is serious bidness. Word done already spread back to the island that I twisted, Diego, and two of his men. I don't know how it made it back there so fast, but it did. But anyway, y'all see that house, right there?" He nodded his head at a two-story, white-bricked house, with a picket fence around it.

Kammron looked out and sized the house up. "Yeah! What about it, Dunn?"

"That mafucka look all nice and cozy and shit from the outside, huh?" Jimmy asked.

Bonkers shrugged his shoulders. "I don't know nigga. What you selling real estate now or some shit?" he questioned growing irritated by the minute.

Now only was his high wearing off, and he was starting to get the itches, but in addition to that he was tired of hearing about Cuba—he was over it.

Jimmy wanted to say something slick, but he held his tongue. "Yo', stay wit' me, I already know both of you, niggas' attention span is shorter than a midget's legs. But you see inside of that house is two assassins that just arrived here from the island. You see the way the heads of Havana do it, they'll send over two killas at first to finish a job. If those two fail they'll send over four. If those four fail, they'll send over eight, then sixteen. Each time they'll double the number of hittas they put on a move until the target is flatlined.

"That's just the way the game goes, by killing Diego we've waged war on his people. The River Boys are 'bout that action, and we have to show them we are, too." He slid the Freddie Krueger mask back over his face and situated the eye holes so he could see. "Let's handle this bidness on some no mercy shit. The whole house gets it—props and all." He grabbed the handle of the door and got ready to get out of the van.

Kammron grabbed his arm. "Hold up, Kid. What the fuck is a prop? And how are we supposed to get inside this house if there are two assassins waiting?" Kammron wasn't afraid, but he wasn't stupid either. He was all about that action, but he wanted to make sure they were handling business in the fashion that they were supposed to be and not ignorantly.

"The Props are how we're about to get in this bitch. Four hoes, Harlem bred, Spanish, and they are probably in there fucking and sucking them two hittas with everything they have because those were my orders. You see when it comes to this game it's all about who you know. What you know and how many people and situations you can control at one time. One false move a peace yo' ass deader than a carcass." He looked over at both men. "Now we about to go in here and shred these niggas in the most sadistic fashion we can think of. The bitches gotta go, too—casualties of war. It's fucked up, but, oh well. It's plenty more hoes where they came from."

"Harlem, nigga. Fuck you mean?" Kammron snapped.

"What?" Jimmy was confused.

"Nigga, you just said them bitches are from Harlem. That they doing you a favor. They riding for the cause and you want us to kill them along with these other two clowns? Yo', my word, that shit foul kid. I don't give a fuck why we hitting them, they still from Harlem."

Bonkers nodded his head. "Yeah, Jimmy, if they rolling wit' you, it ain't no way we can't spare these hoes, and go directly at these niggas? I mean, after all, they riding for the cause, Kid."

Jimmy pulled his mask from his face and looked at Kammron, then over at Bonkers. "Are y'all serious, right now? Saving bitches—really?"

"Harlem, bitches nigga. They ain't just no average hoes from Brooklyn or the Bronx. These is our, hoes." Kammron slid the Black Panther mask over his face.

"Well, muthafuckas hell n'all. Them bitches gotta go because this ain't a game of sparing. We gotta leave that house bloodier than a tampon pulled out of a bitch's pussy on the first day of her cycle. It's as simple as that. The underworld don't respond to warm hearts so y'all shit better turn cold real fast, or you muthafuckas finna be in for a rude awakening. Now let's go in this bitch and chop down everything moving. Guns first, then knives. We out!" He opened the door and jumped out of the minivan.

Bonkers sat there for a minute. He looked over at Kammron. "Yo, what you thinking, Kid?"

Kammron lowered his head and checked to make sure he had the serrated knife inside his black jacket, and both Glocks in his waist. He didn't know how things were going to go down but for some reason, Jimmy insisted they all carry knives.

"Son, I say we go in here and get this shit over with. The faster we handle this bidness, the sooner we can get away from this nigga, and onto something else."

"Yeah, those are my feelings exactly." Bonkers slid his black Power Ranger mask over his face and jumped out of the van beside Kammron.

They rushed to catch up with Jimmy. They found him in the back yard picking up a ladder that had been left on the side of the house by one of the females from Harlem. Jimmy placed the ladder against the side of the house and pointed up to the open window on the second floor. He began to ascend it when he was up a nice distance. Bonkers climbed the ladder next, followed by Kammron.

Jimmy made it to the window and stuck his head inside. He listened to see what he could hear. He heard the sound of music and could smell the heavy scent of perfume in the air. This caused a smile to spread across his lips. He climbed into the house and took his 9mm off his hip. Kammron stepped inside the house, and the heavy scent of perfume wafted to his nose. He took his Glock off his hip and lowered his eyes. His heart began to beat faster and faster. He was in a murderous zone, Bonkers felt the same.

64

Jimmy stepped to the door and eased it open as slowly as possible. He held his breath and stuck his head out, then looked down the hallway. Now he could hear the sounds of Reggae. He saw three females in their panties dancing in the living room. Their backs were to him. They were chilling with a red lightbulb screwed in. He guessed they were dancing in front of the two men that had been sent up from Havana to take him out of the game.

He stepped backward and eased the door closed. "A'ight, they all in the living room. Our Harlem hoes more than likely got their attention doing the usual. Follow my lead!" He pulled three silencers out of his pocket, gave one to each man, and screwed one into his nine. "Let me do the shooting unless you absolutely have too. I need these fuck niggas alive for a minute so they can tell me where exactly this hit is coming from, let's roll."

Kammron didn't like taking orders from Jimmy. He was wishing he would just move out of the way so he and Bonkers could do their thing, but since it was his lick, he decided to let him run the show. Bonkers was ready to get the whole mission over with so he could boost his high. He felt a headache coming on. He frowned under his mask and sniffed hard. He could taste the remnants of the heroin in the back of his throat. He swallowed his saliva and shuddered.

Jimmy eased the door open and got as low to the ground as he could. His shoulder brushed against the wall. His eyes were laser focused on the targets up ahead. When he got closer to the living room where the gathering was taking place, he saw one of the Spanish men laid back on the couch getting head from one of the Harlem freaks. The other one had one of the thick bitches on the table with her legs wide open eating her pussy as if it was his last meal.

There was another female standing in the middle of the floor dancing to Reggae music. She had been the one to pull his coat about the impending arrival of the assassins. Jimmy held his breath and extended his arm. He aimed at the man on the couch getting head and fired his gun two times. The bullets zipped across the room and slammed into his target's shoulder knocking two holes through. The man jumped in the air and pushed the female who had his dick in her mouth away from him, before falling over the back of the couch. The female screamed. This caused the other assassin to jump up and reach for his gun.

Bonkers rushed him with the gun and fired back to back. Sending all his rounds into the man's face ripping it apart. It exploded and left the living room a bloody mess. The assassin's body slumped to the floor. The four females continued to scream at the top of their lungs. Kammron rushed over to the one closest to him and smacked her so hard he knocked her out.

He pointed his gun at the remaining broads. "Say, shorty y'all shut the fuck up. Y'all know what this is, get the fuck on the floor and cover your heads. Now!"

They all followed his directive whimpering and scared for their lives. The Reggae continued to play out of the speakers. Bonkers stood over them trying to decide if he really had it in him to smoke four women on account of the bullshit that Jimmy was talking. As it stood, he didn't think he did. He didn't have a problem smoking a broad, but he tried his best to stay away from doing it to the innocent ones. He figured if Jimmy wanted them taken care of, he was going to have to do it.

Jimmy jumped over the couch and stood in front of the fallen assassin that he'd put two slugs inside of. The man held his shoulder with blood gushing through the cracks of his fingers. He grabbed his legs and pulled him into the front room of the house. Then straddled him and took his knife out of the sheath inside of his jacket.

He spoke to him in Spanish. "Why are you here in America—who sent you?"

The assassin grumbled in pain. His shoulder felt like somebody was digging into it with a screwdriver. "I don't—know—man, I'm jus—just—here-on business."

Jimmy took the knife, slammed it into his collarbone, and twisted it over and over again. The skin ripped, and the interior flesh revealed itself. Blood bubbled around the knife and spilled over. "Who the fuck are you working for?" he asked him again.

The assassin kicked his legs in the air, hollered, and bit into his lip. "Arrgh—stop it—stop it, you son of a bitch!" he snapped in Spanish. "I don't know what you're talking about."

Jimmy cut his left ear off and rubbed it all over his face. "Who the fuck do you work for? Who put the order in for my life?"

The assassin held the side of his face as blood oozed down his chin. "Jimmy Ruiz—you're a—dead man. You—crossed the—the island. You killed—one of—the beloved Princes of the River Boys. Your fate—has already—been set-in-stone. You and everyone—you love—will feel—the wrath of Havana. You can—kill us—today, there will be—twice—as many tomorrow. You'll see—kill me—You—rotten—son—of a bitch!" he demanded, then spat a loogey right in Jimmy's eye and started laughing.

Before the spit could drip off his chin, Jimmy rose the knife high into the air and brought it down at full speed into the assassin's face over and over again. He stabbed and stabbed until his face was unrecognizable. He stood up and aimed his gun down at all four Harlem queens, and pulled the trigger over and over again, murdering them in cold blood. Lastly, he kneeled down beside the first assassin, and cut his throat adding insult to injury.

He looked down at his handy work. "Yo', it's over with! Let's get the fuck out of here."

Chapter 8

Bonkers looked himself over in the full-length mirror and exhaled loudly. "Damn, Kid, I ain't never been this nervous to meet nobody before. I feel like I'm about to be sick, word up."

Kammron came and rested his hand on his shoulder. "Yo', it's cause you're meeting your li'l girl for the first time. You, just like me thought that Yasmin was lying, but DNA don't lie, my nigga. That paper says you're ninety-nine point nine-nine percent the father. That's a hell of a percentage."

Bonkers laughed. "Yeah, dawg, I know. I still can't believe she kept her from me this long. Had I known she was mine I would have made sure she was straight a long time ago. You know I would have."

"Kid, we would have, we brothers, and we in this shit together." Kammron gave him half of hug. "You good to go or what?"

Bonkers shook his head. "I don't know, Dunn. How do I look?"

Kammron looked him over from head to toe. "Yo', you look like a nigga that's about to piss himself. Shorty four, she ain't checking for this Gucci you rocking, Kid. All she wanna know is that you love her and that you gon' be her father from here on out."

"That I am, I just wish we weren't in the middle of a war with them old world Cuban mafuckas. I ain't trying to have my daughter in the middle of no bull shit, and we don't know when they gon clap back. It's been a month, and we ain't heard no noise, but that fool Jimmy is sure it's coming."

Kammron pulled out two Glocks. "Well, when it do we gon' be muthafuckin' ready. Until then we finna make sure Yazzy good to go. Now come on, I think, I just heard some tapping on the door." Kammron stepped out of the room.

Bonkers looked himself over in the mirror again and adjusted the gold ropes around his neck. He was fitted from head to toe in a black and white Gucci fit. His hair was freshly cut. He had on his best Rolex watch and a pair of Gucci frames. If he was going to the club, he woulda passed the bill. He knew he looked good. But he really wondered if he looked well enough for his daughter to accept him.

"Yo', B, they here Kid. Lil mama real pretty, too, she about to knock yo socks off," Kammron promised.

Bonkers took one more deep breath and exhaled. "Yo', I got this. Word to Janine, I got this." He stepped into the hallway and made his way down it. When he got into the front room, he saw that Yasmin held the hand of Yazzy. When Yasmin saw him, she pointed and told Yazzy that he was her father. He felt his heart do a somersault.

Yazzy's eyes got as big as saucers. She smiled and took off running toward him. When she got close enough, she jumped into the air and expected him to catch her which he did. She wrapped her little arms around his neck and rested her face against his. "I love you, daddy, I love you so much!"

Bonkers didn't know what to do or say. But one thing was for sure, as soon as he felt her little arms wrap around his neck he fell in love. "I love you too, Princess. I love you so so much, too." He held her tight and kissed her little cheeks.

Yasmin sat her toiletry bag on the couch. "Look, I know you wanna spend some time with her, and I'm cool with that. If you can just give me a time to come back so I can pick her up that'll be cool wit' me."

Bonkers was too busy looking into Yazzy's eyes. "Man, she's so beautiful. I can't believe this is my baby. To be honest with you I think it's imperative that we all spend some time together. You know to get an understanding amongst ourselves. Kammron gotta handle some bidness with his people today anyway. So, I'm free to chill. What'll you say?"

Yasmin shrugged her shoulders. "I'm not trying to force myself in between y'all relationship. Every little girl needs her father. I know for a fact she needs you. If you'll feel more comfortable with me being there for the first time, then I'm perfectly fine with that. Actually, I think it'll be a great idea. Let me just call my mother and let her know what's good. Hold on a sec." She stepped to the side and did just that.

Kammron came and took hold of Yazzy's little hand. He kissed the back of it, before digging in his pocket and pulling out a hundred-dollar bill. "Here you go li'l, Princess. I know you don't know what to do wit' it yet, but soon you will. I'm your uncle, Kammron, some call me Kamm or Killa. You can call me, Uncle. I want you to know that I love you, and for as long as I'm alive, I'm going to have your back. Do you hear me?" Yazzy turned her head to the side and smiled. She reached out her arms for him. Kammron took her out of Bonkers' arms and hugged her tightly. "Yo she making me fall in love, Bonkers. This gon' be my li'l heart, right here, word up."

Bonkers took her back and nodded. "She got that effect don't she, bruh? This my li'l one, right here, it feels good, Kid."

Yasmin came over and stood beside Bonkers. "Everything is cool on my end. I'm ready to roll out when you're ready."

****

Kammron pulled the black on black Mustang to the curb and beeped the horn. It was four in the afternoon, and it was time for him to pick up both Shelly and Shana from the beauty salon. He'd dropped them off at seven o'clock that morning and still couldn't believe it took them nearly nine hours to get their hair done. That was crazy for him to believe, when it came to Shelly, he made sure he got her hair done at least once a month. Her eyebrows, fingers, and toes were done every other week. He knew that if he wanted to keep on having a bad woman he had to foot the bill. That's just the way the game went.

Shana was the first to emerge out of the shop with her hair blowing behind her. She wore a tight-fitting Prada skirt dress that hung to her curves. He recognized it right away. It had been a number that he'd bought for Shelly a few summers back. Shana was always wearing Shelly's clothes.

Shana came to the car, sat in the passenger's seat, and closed the door. "She still got about fifteen minutes before she comes out. She getting new micro braids."

"Yo', get ya ass in the backseat, shorty. The passenger's seat is reserved for, my bitch only. You ain't that."

Shana felt a twinge of hurt. "Damn, Killa, why you gotta treat me so harshly all of the time? I ain't seen you in a few days and I just wanted to chill up here wit' you until she comes out of the shop. I mean, it is gon' take fifteen minutes. We can roll around for at least ten of those minutes and I can thank you for getting my hair, and nails did." She rubbed her freshly manicured nails over the front of his pants and clutched his dick. Within a matter of seconds, it proceeded to rise. This made her smile.

Kammron looked past her shoulder and pushed her hand away. "How you know it's gon' take fifteen more minutes? That's what her beautician told you or something?" He peeped the way her skirt pulled back to expose her thick, chocolate thighs. They looked smooth and delectable.

She caught his eyes trained on her and shivered. Then she opened her thighs wider forcing the skirt to travel upward a bit more. "Yeah, she actually said twenty," she lied. "But I know it's going to take at least fifteen. Plus, she telling her a long ass story and that makes her keep on stopping and shit. You know how that goes." She squeezed his dick again. "I could take care of you real quick. Yo', dick way too hard to say no, anyway. Plus, I ain't heard my sister moaning all loud and shit in a long time." She opened her thighs as wide as she could and rubbed her fingers along the front of her panties.

Kammron saw the plump lips appear through the fabric. He sent Shelly a text telling her he was about to take Shana to get something to eat, and they would be back in twenty minutes. Then he turned on the ignition and drove away from the curb.

Shana reached over, unzipped his pants, fished his big dick out, and stroked it up and down, before sliding her mouth over it. In a matter of seconds, she was making loud sucking noises that were driving him crazy. She knelt on the seat and really went to work. Her skirt pulled up along the small of her back. The white boy short panties were deep within the crease of her ass.

Kammron rubbed the chocolate moons and squeezed them. "Shorty, I'm finna fuck yo' li'l ass, I can't take it no more. You keep playing wit' me, too much." He rubbed her pussy and smashed the juicy lips together.

Shana sucked him harder, trying to remember how the porn stars had done it on the videos she watched. She often practiced on a pickle while watching them. She pumped her fist up and down his piece and sucked hard on the head.

"Mmm, on my mother, I'm finna wear that ass out." He was looking around for a place to park. Finally settling on the parking lot of the old railway yard right off Lennox. He pulled the car to the end of it and parked alongside a big dumpster. "Bitch get yo lil ass in that back, I'm finna take that cherry. Word up."

Shana's coochie was oozing as she climbed into the back seat. Once there she laid on her back, opened her thighs wide and rubbed her bald pussy. She opened the lips for him to see her business. "You want some of this, daddy, huh?"

Kammron crawled between her thighs and lowered himself down to her coochie lips. He kissed them and licked up and down her slit. She shivered against him, moaned, and pinched her nipples through her dress. Kammron continued to munch, sucking hard on her clitoris.

"Fuck me, Killa, please daddy—it's time. Fuck me, right now," she begged.

Kammron stroked his dick five times, and placed the head on her sex lips, before sinking into her entrance.

"Uhhhh—Killa!" Shana screamed.

Kammron wasn't trying to hear nothing, he fucked her as hard as he could until he broke through the barrier of her hymen. His dick sunk as far into her as it could go, then he was fuckin' her at full speed holding her by the thighs. Her pussy felt like a velvet fist and was hot, and meaty. He went into overdrive trying to get his nut as the car rocked back and forth.

"Un-un-un, Kamm! Ooo, daddy—daddy, ooo, I knew it! I knew it, oooo, it hurts but it feels so good. Harder daddy!" She held his waist and closed her eyes as he pounded her lil pussy with long strokes. The width of him stretched her walls, and his length pounded at the road that led into her stomach.

Kammron sucked her neck and pumped his hips faster, and harder. Their middles clapped loudly. The scent of their sex rose in the car. Her pussy felt like it got better and better with each stroke. He couldn't take it, he felt his nut building, it was only a matter of time. He sped up and diddled her clitoris while he stroked her.

Shana screeched and tightened her thighs around his waist. She tilted her head back and screamed again. "Uhhhh-shit,

Killa, I'm cumming like my, sister! I'm cumming like my, sister, uhhh fuck!" She fell on her back and came hard all over him.

Kammron humped harder and felt his climax approaching. He sucked on the side of her neck as his nut shot out of him, and into her womb. He jerked, stabbed, shivered, and pumped faster until his dick became too sensitive to move it. He kept himself planted deep within the essence of her cave. "Yo', you say something to your sister about this and on my mother, I'ma twist you, shorty." He didn't know if he really would, but he felt the need to scare her mouth shut. Shana could be a bit of a Yenta, a big mouth.

Shana rubbed all over his chest. "I promise, I ain't gon' say nothing. Just please fuck me from time to time. I always knew you was gon' be my first. Ever since I was ten years old, I just knew it." She rose, kissed his lips, licked all over them, and moaned into his mouth. "We better get the fuck out of here. And roll down these windows because she gon' be able to smell our scents, and that'll make her go—"

Urrrrr-uh! Was the sound of black Suburban slamming on its brakes in the parking lot forty feet away from them. Kammron peeked and saw what time it was. He dived to the front seat and grabbed his Glock.

"Shana get down!"

Two Cubans jumped out of the truck with assault rifles in their hands. They stopped, aimed at the Mustang and shots were fired.

Boom! Boom! Boom! Boom!

The windows to the Mustang began to shatter around them. They could hear the constant *tink! tink, tink,* of the bullets hitting the metal. Shana screamed as Kammron's cum seeped out of her vagina's folds. Kammron grabbed the

Glock, opened the driver's door, and fell on the ground. Once out he scrambled to the hood of the car and bussed over it.

Bocka! Bocka! Bocka! Bocka!

The Cubans jumped back and continued to spray the Mustang until their rifles clicked empty. As soon as they were, they jumped inside of the Suburban and screeched away with smoke coming from their tires.

****

Bonkers held Yazzy in his arms as he carried her down the hallway to Yasmin's mother's crib. He stood and waited for her to open the door. Yasmin opened it and stood to the side for him to enter the small Project apartment. He carried Yazzy inside. The first thing he noticed was that they didn't have any furniture, other than a floor model television set that a more smaller thirteen-inch color television was sitting on. He surmised that the floor model was broken, and they used it for a stand. It was typical Project living.

"Yo, where do you want me to lay her?"

Yasmin held up a finger. "Hold on, let me go and get a blanket then we can lay her on the floor on a pallet." She disappeared toward the back of the house.

Bonkers looked around and saw how many roaches were crawling and imagined that there had to be rats somewhere close and frowned. He was looking so evil by the time Yasmin came back that she grew worried.

"Say, what's the matter, Dunn?" She asked setting the blanket in the floor and then placing a sheet on top of it.

He peeped the roaches again. "Yo, now that I know she really my kid, I can't have her staying here. Especially not on no pallet with gang banging ass roaches only a few feet away and approaching. I'm more of a man than that. Why don't y'all

76

just come back to my crib for the night, then tomorrow while I take her shopping you can browse the web for a place for y'all to move into. I'll pay up the first six months of rent and we'll go from there until you can get on your feet. How does that sound?"

Yasmin scrunched her face. "Bonkers, I didn't fight for her to be a part of your life, so you could take pity on me. I know this may not be the best living arrangement but I'm trying to figure things out and get myself together so that I don't have to depend on anybody." She reached for Yazzy.

Bonkers took a step back still holding her. "Shorty that ain't finna happen. You finna bring ya ass to my crib tonight. Sleep peacefully, then tomorrow we'll make a decision of what we're going to do as co-parents. Tonight, you ain't got a fuckin' choice, though. I don't take pity on nobody, but I'm her daddy, and this ain't what's up, deal wit' it. My baby deserves the best, that's just all there is to it."

Yasmin stared at him for a long time, then looked around at the empty apartment. She felt pity for herself. That was no way to live. Not only did Yazzy deserve better, but she did as well. "You know what, Bonkers, I ain't gon' argue wit' you. Let me get a few things and we can be out."

Coke Kings

Chapter 9

Early the next morning Kammron rushed over to Bonkers Project apartment and beat on the door. *Bomp! Bomp! Bomp! Bomp! Bomp!* He was breathing heavy, high as a kite and ready to murder something. He needed to know why Bonkers had neglected to answer his phone all night or not cared to respond to his urgent messages. The heat was on and his right-hand man hadn't been there holding his torch beside him. He beat on the door some more. *Bomp! Bomp! Bomp! Bomp!*

Bunkers hopped up from the couch and threw the sheet off of him. He slid his hand under the couch and grabbed his Glock, cocked it, and flicked it off of safety. He placed his back to the door. "Yo', who the fuck is it beating on my muthafuckin' door like you crazy?" he hollered.

Yasmin stuck her head out the door of the bedroom. He waved her to go back inside of it.

Now Kammron was wishing he wouldn't have forgotten his spare key to Bonkers' crib. He'd been in such a haste to get out of the house that he'd left it in the top drawer. "Yo', it's me, nigga, open the mafuckin' door." He punched it.

Bonkers slid to the peephole and looked out of it. He saw Kammron standing in front of the door with a mug on his caramel face. He slid off the chain and pulled the door open. "What's good, Kid?"

Kammron flew past him. "Yo, why the fuck you ain't answer, your phone yesterday, Kid? You ain't respond to a nigga texts or nothing." He was heated. He mugged Bonkers before turning his back to him.

Bonkers closed the door and locked it back. "I was spending time wit' my daughter all day and night, Son. I turned that boy off. I wasn't trying to have no distractions. I don' already missed four years of her life man."

T.J. Edwards

Kammron waved him off. "Dunn, I get all of that, but that don't mean we ain't beefing wit' these punk ass Cubans. Yo', I swear to, Kathy, that I wanna wipe all them bitches off the face of the earth."

Bonkers looked him up and down. "Yo' what the fuck happened to you? Hold on, let me get you something to drink." He rushed to the refrigerator and brought back a fruit punch juice.

Kammron took it. "Thanks, B."

"A'ight, now tell me what's good?"

Kammron opened the juice and sat on the couch. He took a long swallow from it, drinking it down halfway. "They made a play on my life yesterday, God. Caught me jumping out of Shana's pussy in the parking lot of the old railway yard. Bitches woulda killed both of us if I hadn't been bucking back at 'em. They Swiss-cheesed the Mustang. That bitch looks like Queen Latifah's whip in the movie *'Set It Off'* after they blazed her ass.

Bonkers was vexed. "Yo, what's good? We can go handle them, boys, right now. Let me go and get my gats, I'll be right back." He got ready to rush to the back room when Yazzy came out of it running down the hallway. Yasmin tried to stop her. When she saw Bonkers she jumped, and he pulled her into his arms. "What's the matter, baby?"

Yazzy hugged his neck as hard as she could. "I love you, daddy, I was missing you."

Bonkers felt his cold heart melt. He kissed her and held her to his chest. "I love you, so much li'l mama. I'm right here and I ain't going nowhere Daddy promise."

She planted kisses all over his cheeks. "Daddy, can I go wit' you today?"

She sat back and looked into his eyes with her baby browns.

80

Kammron jumped up heated. While he felt good for Bonkers now that he had finally connected with his daughter. He felt like beating into the young man's head that the world wasn't going to stop because he was a newly found father, and neither were their enemies. He felt that Bonkers had to get with the program, or they were going to be ass out.

Yasmin made her way down the hallway with a robe tied around her. She sauntered into the kitchen and poured herself a glass of tap water. "Good morning, everybody." She took a sip of the water, feeling refreshed and energized after not having to sleep on a roach-infested floor for a night. That coupled with the fact that Bonkers was promising to help better her and Yazzy's situation allowed her to have one of the best night sleeps of her life.

"Yo', hell n'all, Dunn! So, what she staying wit' you now? Y'all a couple and some shit?" Kammron really didn't care but he was heated anyway so he was looking for somebody to take his anger and frustration out on and Yasmin seemed like an easy target since he couldn't attack Yazzy's situation.

Yasmin's mood instantly fell to that of a depressive one. "Nah, he just let us stay here for the night," she mumbled and lowered her head.

Bonkers shot daggers at Kammron. "Yo', chill, God. Shorty straight, I ain't want them staying in that roach, and the rat-infested apartment they were staying in, so they're here. Nigga, fall back I got this shit over here. Word up."

Kammron mugged him. "Yeah, well that shit cool, but we got bidness to take care of. We gotta get out of here and do what we gotta do, so let's get a move on." He pulled a rolled Dutch out of his pocket and sparked the blunt. Then blew big puffy clouds to the ceiling and inhaled the gray smoke hard.

Yasmin stepped to Bonkers and leaned into his ear. "It's clear ya man's ain't feeling this whole situation. Maybe me and Yazzy should leave? We ain't trying to cause no trouble."

Yasmin was playing the mental manipulation game. She felt that it would be smart for her to drive a wedge in between Kammron and Bonkers so that Bonkers could focus more on his fatherly roll with their daughter, and there may even been potential for them to rekindle some of the old flames. She felt that as long as Kammron was in the picture there would always be some kind of drama, and bullshit popping off. Things that would disrupt their stability.

"What? Man, ex that shorty, I'm my own man. I already told you what it was. You gon' jump yo ass on that laptop back there and search until you find some places to move into. Places that ain't the fuckin' Projects. That's your task for the day after you cook up some breakfast for the crib. I'll leave you to it." He pointed toward the kitchen.

Yasmin smiled weakly and headed into the kitchen opening the refrigerator again to see what she was about to prepare. As she searched her mind started to compute ways to get in between the two men. A sinister smile spread across her lips.

Bonkers placed Yazzy on her feet. "Baby, Daddy, has to go to work with your uncle today. When I get back home me, and you are going to spend some more time together. Do you understand me?"

She turned her head sideways. "What understand mean?" Yazzy asked.

"It means, uh—" He rubbed his head and tried to come up with a way to explain it to her better.

Yasmin came and took her hand. "It means that Daddy wanted you to know what he's going to do today. He wanted to tell you because you're special."

Yazzy looked back at Bonkers, yanked her hand away from Yasmin, and rushed to Bonkers hugging his legs again, until he picked her up, and planted kisses all over her.

****

Three hours later Jimmy was sitting in the backseat of the stolen Yukon Denali with black leather gloves on his hand, and a Jason mask on his face. He was dressed in all black just like Bonkers, and Kammron. Each man had on white Jason masks. Jimmy looked out at the small Cuban restaurant. "Once we do this shit it's gon' make the old-world turn-up, bruh. Inside of this joint is some of the heads from Havana. They are directly connected with the River Boys. This punk ass restaurant is a front. It is used as a command center for Cuba to orchestrate hits, money washing, and narcotics distribution from, right here in New York. We go in here and wreck this shit, we take a direct shot at Havana. With that being said are you li'l niggas really sure y'all ready to do this?"

Kammron cocked his Mac-11. "Yo, fuck these cats, B, let's handle this bidness, and get this shit over with. They took a shot at my life the other night, I ain't been right, since. I ain't with this paranoid shit. Besides, I'm sure that was the Suburban that rolled up on, me and Shana. Look it still got the bullet holes on the side of it." Kammron pointed toward the truck that was parked just two spaces over from them.

Bonkers cocked his Tech. "The faster we get in, the faster we can get back out. We wetting everythang, or is this just to send a message to the shooters that hollered at, bruh?"

Kammron snapped. "Aw hell n'all, nigga, I'm wetting every fuckin' thing, and smoking every nigga up in this, bitch. Fuck sending a message, my message gon' be get the caskets! That's just that."

Jimmy was already tired of Kammron and his ridiculous temper. He hated how Kammron always seemed to act out of emotion instead of intelligence. He knew Kammron had no idea what he was really up against, and while he wanted to take the two minutes to explain to him what it really was, he didn't have the patience to do so.

"Yo', if that's what it is then let's handle bidness accordingly. It's after ten now which means the bosses are meeting. When we first go inside there are going to be a series of old-world bodyguards standing around on security. The four bosses of New York will more than likely be sitting around the table discussing politics. The front entrance will be heavily guarded, but there are windows in the front of the establishment as well. I say Bonkers you chop that bitch down. Meanwhile Kammron you'll go through the back door or the joint where the dishwashers enter and exit. You run up in that bitch with gun blazing and cut up anything in your path."

"And what the fuck you gon' be doing?" Kammron asked.

"I'm gon' wait at the side door if anybody should escape. I'll be standing right there ready to put more slugs in their ass than a crazed lunatic." Jimmy smiled under his mask.

Bonkers kept seeing images of Yazzy in his brain. He missed her already. He even found himself thinking about Yasmin as well. He shook his head. "Yo', whatever man, let's handle this bidness and be the fuck out." He opened the driver's door and jumped out of the truck with the Tech in hand.

He stayed low to the ground, traveled alongside a doughnut shop that was two establishments away from the Cuban restaurant. On the way there a man came from the side door of the doughnut shop with a bag of garbage in his hand. When he saw Bonkers wearing the mask, and the gun in his hand, he dropped the garbage and attempted to turn around so he could run back into the shop when Bonkers grabbed him around the neck from the back.

"Oh, no you don't." He proceeded to choke him out as hard as he could while the man fought against him struggling to breathe. Harder and harder he squeezed for a full minute.

They fell to the ground, and still Bonkers did not let him go. By the time life left the man four minutes had passed. Bonkers stood up and looked down on his victim remorseless. He rushed to the front of the business and jogged over to the Cuban restaurant. He stood and aimed his gun at the glass and began spraying with no mercy.

Pow! Pow! Pow! Pow!

The glass exploded and spilled into the interiors of the restaurant. Bonkers' bullets hit two of the bosses right away, causing chest shots that took their lives immediately. He continued to spray with the Tech-9 jumping in his hand.

Whoom!

Kammron kicked in the back door to the Cuban restaurant. He rushed into the kitchen with his Mac-11 at the ready. The workers began to scatter and duck for cover. He began to pick them a part one by one.

Pop! Pop! Pop! Pop!

He spent shells out of the Mac and rolled across the floor as his bullets found entrances to the many bodies. In a matter of seconds, the kitchen was filled with smoke and gunpowder. He continued to shoot, made his way to the front of the restaurant where he could see Bonkers' bullets shredding the place. One of the bosses low crawled on his elbows. He positioned himself under a table and pulled out his cellphone. Before he could dial the first number Kammron aimed and lit his ass up like a Christmas tree. Five shots directly through the side of the jaw that left him twisted.

Jimmy could hear the rapid shots going off. He smiled and lowered his eyes. He knew what was to come next. All he had to do was wait. He stood on the side of the door and waited for Mark. He was sure he would take the side door just like they'd previously discussed. More shots were fired. Somebody screamed out in pain. Jimmy could tell who it was, but he hoped and prayed it wasn't Mr. Marotta himself. That would spoil everything he was sure, he waited impatiently.

"Come on—come on," he grumbled. As if his prayer was being answered the side door flew open, and blindly Mark ran out of it, and right into Jimmy's chest. Jimmy snatched him up. "Be quiet muthafucka, run that way. I'll meet up wit' you later."

Mark was shaking like crazy as he recognized Jimmy's voice. He shook his head, then Jimmy's hand. "Thank you, thank you, you won't regret this." Then he was running away from the scene of the massacre.

Chapter 10

"Kamm, yo ass is too much. What the hell are you about to do with a Porsche?" Shelly asked, walking behind Kammron in the Porsche dealership.

"Yo', what the fuck am I not going to do in a Porsche, Goddess? I been grinding as hard as I can for three months straight. I got a li'l paper tucked away from fucking wit' Jimmy. I think it's time to jump in a Porsche. A mafucka deserve this, so fall back and just watch how daddy ball." Kammron said carrying the Gucci book bag filled with a hundred thousand dollars cash.

He wasn't thinking about leasing nothing. He was on some boss shit. Pure cash, under the table, he wanted to get it done. He spotted a black on black Porsche, with the red leather interior circled around it and started to smiled. He removed the Gucci shades from his face and kissed the hood.

"The Kid want this mafucka, right here. This me, right here, word to Kathy." He pulled open the door, sat behind the steering wheel, took a whiff of the leather, and started cheesing. He began blowing the horn over and over again.

The dealer jogged out of the building with his suit jacket blowing in the wind. He rushed over to the Porsche and placed his hand on the hood. "Son, hey, may I help you?" he hollered already irritated.

Kammron stepped out of the Porsche and looked the white man over. He was dressed in a snug-fitting business suit. His face was redder than a lobster. "Yo', say my man tell the God what he gotta do to roll off the lot with this joker, right here?"

The dealer looked him up and down. "Son, I don't think this is the vehicle for you unless you're ready to drop eighty thousand dollars." He sized Kammron up. He was seconds away from calling security to get him off of his lot.

Kammron dusted his Gucci fit off. "Say, Money, why don't you go in the office, and get the keys so we can take this joker for a test drive. The Kid, wants this whip, right here and whatever I want I get."

The dealer backed up and grew worried. "What you saying, Kid? You shaking me down or something?"

Kammron laughed, then slammed the book bag on the hood of the car and unzipped it. "Check this out, Playboy. This is New York, I'm from the finest borough of them all, Harlem. Now I got a hunnit gees in this bag, and it's yours. All I want is this black bitch, right here."

The dealer looked him over closely. "Somebody send you, to me? What makes you think I'll take cash for one of these here Porsches instead of going through the proper procedures?"

Kammron laughed. "First of all, the God don't get down like that. Secondly, the sticker price is eighty gees. I'm throwing you twenty extra just to fuck wit' me. I don't care what you do wit' it long as this black bitch come wit' me when it's all said and done." He placed the bag to the dealer's chest. "Whatta you say, homie?"

The dealer looked into the bag and saw all of the money. He could smell the bills. Twenty thousand dollars was a hell of a payoff to accept cash for one of his Porsches. Business had been a bit slow as of late, and it was time to make ends meet. He didn't want to go back to North Carolina having failed to make it in the Big Apple. "Son, step into my office, we got some thangs that we need to discuss." He adjusted his suit coat and led Kammron across the parking lot.

****

Bonkers pushed Yazzy's swing and shielded the sun by use of his hand. He surveyed the park closely, on the lookout for any potential threats to himself, or his baby girl. There was a full court game of basketball going on behind him. To his right, there was a bunch of people set up on the picnic tables eating barbecue and laughing out loud. To his left was the parking lot.

Yasmin came over and handed him a cold Apple juice. "Here you go, Bonkers. This heat kicking my butt, I know it gotta be kicking yours, too." She wiped a trace of sweat off her forehead and exhaled loudly.

Bonkers took the drink and continued pushing Yazzy on the swing. "Damn, ma, you coulda opened it for a nigga." He handed it back to her.

She laughed and opened the top, then gave it back to him. "Here you go your, Majesty." She rolled her eyes.

He took a long swallow. "Stop playing, Goddess. You know you love serving a nigga." He glanced over to the project buildings and looked up and down them, then to Yazzy. She had a big smile on her face simply enjoying her father pushing her swing back and forth. Bonkers sighed. "Yo', I gotta get her out of here man. She shouldn't be in no hood. My baby deserves to be out of the ghetto all together. I gotta make it happen for her. I been thinking about going to a technical college or something. You know getting myself one of those degrees. That way I can provide her with a better life." He looked down at Yazzy again.

The sight of her long hair that was done up with Barrets warmed his heart. He didn't even know he was fiending for a daughter until she became part of his life.

Yasmin smiled. "I think you should, I know a few people around the way that are getting degrees in all sorts of things. Once they get them, they are making a nice amount of legal money. Providing their families with futures. I been thinking that I wanna better myself as well. I mean why can't both of Yazzy's parents get their stuff together? If we do, we can provide her with the best possible life she deserves. Bonkers I just want us to work together. I can't do this on my own. I'm not afraid to tell you that I need you. Not afraid to let you know that I'm afraid to do this alone. Like, I'm willing to do whatever it takes to get right with you, Bonkers. I don't want her living in a broken home." Though Yasmin meant every word she said to him, she knew it was imperative to keep the conversation steered in the direction of Yazzy. Yazzy seemed to be Bonkers' weakness.

Bonkers pushed Yazzy's swing again and allowed it to move back and forth. He was slightly confused as to what Yasmin was trying to say, but he thought he had an inkling. "Shorty, ever since you've known me I've always been an uncut typa nigga that don't sugar coat shit." He mentally chastised himself for cursing around his baby girl. Told himself that he had to get better with his speech around her. Her ears were those of Angels. "What I mean is, I need you to come right out and say what you trying to say. You ain't gotta beat around the bush."

Yasmin felt her stomach turn over. "Look, Bonkers, I still like you a whole lot, and it's clear that our daughter loves you with her whole heart. Every time she sees you she lights up. She wakes up crying out for you already, and the two of you look absolutely amazing together. I don't want to break up that dynamic." She searched his face closely. She could see the emotion written across it when she spoke about Yazzy. Now it was time to bring it home. She knew Bonkers was a Lion, outside of Kammron he hated other men. It was time to bring out the big guns. "What, I'm saying is, I don't want to bring another man into the picture. I don't need her bonding with no other male. You can't trust these dudes out here, Bonkers, they ain't right. If somebody hurt our baby, man I'd—"

Bonkers felt like he was ready to kill a thousand people with his bare hands. "Man, I wish you would bring another nigga around my, Jewel. I'll smoke that nigga, and you. I'm not finna play about, my baby, and you're her mother, I'm not finna play about you either," he snapped.

Yasmin took a step back in defense. She wanted to smile, and it was so hard to not do exactly that. But she knew she had to stay in her role. "Bonkers, I would never, I respect you so much more than that. But what do I do when I feel lonely like I already am? I'm tired of being unprotected. I miss the feel of a man since I had, Yazzy, I've been celibate."

Bonkers nearly broke his neck to look in her direction. "Yo', Yasmin, you already know I'ma street nigga. I ain't ready for all that one on one, Goddess. I just don't think, I'm that mature. But looking at this baby girl, right here, I can't help but see you in her. I can't love her without making sure you're straight at all costs. I don't know what that means relationship-wise, but I got love for you, Shorty. I'ma make sure you're good, trust me."

Yasmin smiled. "I do trust you. You're probably the only man I trust in this world." She stepped next to him and hugged his waist. "Thank you, too."

Bonkers wrapped his arm around her. "Thank me for what?"

"For being a man, for accepting me along with our daughter. It takes one hell of a man to do just that. I appreciate you, Bonkers, I swear I do."

Bonkers hugged her body and kissed her in the side of the forehead. "I appreciate you for giving me such a beautiful, baby. I'm sorry I denied her for so long. You was—" He caught himself and looked down at Yazzy. "Let's just say I was bogus. You deserved better treatment than that."

She shrugged her shoulders. "We're still kids, Bonkers. I forgive you, baby. Let's just promise to do better, okay." She kissed his cheek and smiled.

"I promise ma, word to, Janine I promise." He picked Yazzy up out of the swing and wrapped his arm around Yasmin's neck. "Yo', let's roll out to Coney Island. Have a li'l family time for a few hours. What you think?"

Yasmin didn't know what it meant, but she felt giddy. "That sounds amazing, Bonkers, let's do it."

****

Kammron punched the gas and exceeded his speeds to a hundred and ten on the interstate. He turned up the bottle of Moët, and took a long swallow from it, pushing the pedal to the floor, weaving in and out of traffic.

Shelly sat in the passenger's seat feeling like she was about to lose her mind. She thought Kammron was a maniac, she covered her eyes. "Killa, please slow yo' ass down. You finna give me a heart attack. I swear to God I'm not lying." She opened her eyes to see him speed around a Jeep in just the nick of time. She closed her eyes back tightly.

Kammron laughed. "Yo', I'm rolling a fuckin' Porsche. I'm on my, boss shit. The road belongs to me. Fuck the world, it belongs to Harlem, Goddess. What the deal?" he hollered. He flew past a state trooper doing a hundred and ten and flicked him off.

The trooper turned on his lights and jumped in hot pursuit of him. Ordering cars to pull to the side of the road. The sun was just beginning to set behind the clouds. The interstate had mild traffic.

Kammron looked over his shoulder. He laughed and turned the Moët up again. "Fuck the world, Son ain't finna fuck in mine, trust me!" He punched the Porsche and took it to top speeds.

Then he began zigging and zagging in traffic, before taking an exit, instead of slowing his pace he kept his foot in the pedal, zipped through the red lights, and nearly was sideswiped by a garbage truck.

Shelly screamed.

Kammron laughed at the top of his lungs. His suicidal feeling coming on heavy. He turned the bottle of Moët back up, finished it, and threw it out of the driver's window. "This shit feels good. Yo Shelly suck my dick!"

"What?"

He began unbuckling his Gucci belt. "You heard me, suck this mafucka—now!" He pulled it out and it was rock hard from the excitement, then he let his seat back.

Shelly looked over their shoulder to see how close the troopers were. She could see the bright lights from their sirens about a half of block back. Kammron jumped back onto the interstate, storming.

"Kamm, this is nuts."

He laughed. "I know shorty, and that's why I'm trying to buss one. Come on and hit, Papi off, hurry up!" He reached out for her and tangled his fingers in her hair.

She smacked his hand away, terrified. "Kamm, if you kill us, I swear to God I'ma get you back." She promised as dumb as that sounded.

"Shorty, you good, I got this mafucka." He peeked into his rearview mirror and saw that he was creating a healthy distance from the troopers.

Shelly's mouth engulfed his penis, she sucked it tight and fast. Then added plenty of spit just the way he liked it. Every time his head hit the back of her throat she gagged but kept right on sucking.

"Mmm, that's what I'm talking about, shorty. That's how you treat a God." He punched the accelerator and fucked hard into her mouth. *'There's no way the troopers are going to get anywhere near close to me. After all, I'm swerving a muthafuckin' Porsche,'* he thought.

Chapter 11

Bonkers kissed Yazzy on the forehead and pulled the covers snuggly over her body. He plugged in the night light and started the soft jazz she'd become accustomed to falling asleep too. Then he stepped into the hallway and pulled her door close. When he got back into the living room, he saw Yasmin filling their Champagne glasses with Dom Perignon.

"What you in here doing, li'l lady?" He laughed.

"Well, seeing as this is my first apartment. A long way from the ghetto. My daughter is safe and away from—"

"Our daughter," Bonkers interrupted her.

"Sorry, seeing how our daughter is safe, and away from harm. You and I have been co-parenting for a month now without so much as a fight. I think it causes for celebration." She handed him the glass and smiled. Her Chanel perfume drifted from her soft skin and floated to his nostrils. She smelled good to him.

Bonkers took the glass and clinked it against hers. "Cheers shorty." He downed the Champagne and smacked his lips. Then set the glass on the counter and pulled her into his embrace. "Yo, word to Janine, I appreciate you, Goddess. Every time I think about what you musta went through trying to take care of her on your own it just makes me feel some type of way. I just wish I would have really known way back when, damn, but I apologize. I really mean that." He looked into her caramel brown eyes with sincerity.

Yasmin got lost in his for a moment. She seemed under his spell. She smiled and eased out of his embrace. "It's fine Bonkers, you can't be held accountable for something you didn't even know. The fact that you've been consistent ever since those test results came back says a lot about your character. I am honored to call you her father. Honored to be co-parenting with you." She turned to take a seat on the blanket she'd placed on the floor for comfort.

This was her second day inside her new apartment, and even though she didn't have any furniture just yet. She felt good to have her own residence outside of the ghetto. Bonkers paid up the rent for a full six months. The utilities were included, so all she had to do was furnish it, and find a place of employment to keep things moving forward after the six months ran their course.

Bonkers grabbed her waist and brought her back to him. He walked backward until her back was against the wall. He rested his forehead against hers and took a hold of her ass. "Say, Goddess, I been thinking about us raising our baby together instead of apart. Every time I look at her, I see you, and every time I look at you I see the woman who gave my Shorty life. You got me feeling some type of way. I been fiending for you for an entire week now."

Yasmin batted her eyelashes. "Just a week?" she teased, as his hands roamed all over her ass squeezing.

Bonkers laughed. "That's all I'm willing to admit, too." He leaned his head down and kissed her soft lips. They felt like moist pillows.

"Mmm, baby," Yasmin moaned.

Her tongue lashed out at his. They twirled round and round each other. She wrapped her arms around his neck and intensified the kiss. Bonkers gripped that ass that was encased inside a pair of tight Jordache jeans. It felt round and soft, hot to the touch. He ran his tongue up and down her neck and bit into the soft skin there.

Yasmin moaned again, "I want you, Bonkers, it's been so long, but I want you tonight."

Bonkers was already throbbing in his pants. He kissed her more passionately and led her to the blanket. Once there he sat

Coke Kings

down and allowed her to straddle his waist. He waited excit-
edly in anticipation. She climbed over his waist staring him in
the eyes. Then they were making out as if they were in high
school, breathing heavy and panting, it felt like their first time.
Bonkers broke the kiss and looked up to her. "I gotta have
some of this body, too, baby." He flipped her onto her back,
unbuttoned her pants, pulled them down her thick thighs, and
off of her ankles, then tossed them aside. "Open these legs."
He crawled between them and planted kisses all over her panty
front while rubbing her sex through the panties.

Yasmin humped into his hand. She could feel her juices
pouring into her panties already. "Unnhhh, Bonkers. What are
you going to do to me?" She sucked her bottom lip and
moaned again.

Bonkers pulled her panties down to her knees and pushed
her thighs to her chest. His face appeared in her center. He
eyed her juicy pussy, licked the chubby lips, then trailed his
tongue up and down her slit, before sucking each individual
lip.

She arched her back and moaned loudly, "Shit, baby-
awww-aww-aww. It feels so good!"

He sucked on her clitoris, and slipped two fingers into her
hole, running them in and out at full speed. Her kitty began to
ooze around his digits. He slurped up her essence and swallowed it on his grown man shit.

Yasmin purred. She sucked her finger into her mouth and
licked all over it. The pure freak ready to rear its beastly head.
"Unnhhh—it feels so good, Bonkers!"

Bonkers didn't mind eating the pussy but he wanted to
fuck something. It had been a long time since he'd gotten between Yasmin's thighs. He wanted to change that. He stripped
down and got back between them, tossed her right thigh on his
shoulder, and eased into her tight pussy. His eyes rolled into

the back of his head the deeper he traveled into her hot pocket. When his stomach rested against her he knew he'd hit soft bottom. He told himself to beat that shit up, cocked back, slammed forward as hard as he could and repeated the process until he had a steady rhythm going. He fucked her so hard they were sliding across the floor. The sound of their skin erupted as they slapped into each other.

"Uh-uh-uhh-uhhh-uhhhh—Bonkers! Yes-yes-yes, baby-ooo—fuck yes!" she gasped wrapping her thighs around his body.

Bonkers marveled at the way his dick looked going in and out of her pussy. Every time he pulled back far enough it would expose her pink insides. When he moved forward his pelvis would smash her juicy lips. Their connection looked glorious to him. Her heat was too much. He sped up the pace, pushed his hands under her blouse and pulled it over her head. He unsnapped her bra from the front, her B cups spilled out. A few stretch marks decorated the globes. In Bonkers' eyes that just meant they were real titties. His dick got harder as he sucked all over them and fucked her as hard as he could.

Yasmin dug her nails into his back and dragged them across it. She couldn't help it, his dick was way too long, and wide. She could barely take it, but then he flipped her on her stomach and slid back in. From this angle, he was able to hit her G-spot back to back.

She crawled to her knees and forced her ass back into him again and again. "Fuck me, baby—fuck me harder! Aww my, God, this is your pussy—it's yours." She closed her eyes and grabbed a fist full of the blanket for no reason at all. It was just that the dick was so good.

Bonkers licked all over the back of her neck and continued to pound her out. "It's us, baby-aarggh, you hear me! Me and you—us." He sped up the pace again.

Yasmin tried her best to smile before she hollered out she was cumming, and cumming hard. She fell to her stomach and started quivering with Bonkers behind her long stroking her like a stallion. She could hear the sounds of her suction as he traveled in and out of her, breathing heavy. He bit the back of her neck again like a Pit Bull and came hard shooting into her tight womb.

She felt the jolts of his semen and felt another orgasm mounting. "Uhhhh—uhhhh, I love you Bonkers-shit!" she screamed cumming harder than before.

Bonkers didn't know what to say to that, so instead of speaking, he flipped her over, and tongued her down, while he slow stroked her pussy. "You're my, baby, mine. This my pussy, tell me it's mine!" he growled.

Yasmin's eyes rolled into the back of her head now. She felt possessed. "It's yours, baby—it's yours."

****

Mark Maratto stood at the head of the conference table, all five feet four inches of him. He looked down the long expanse of the table into a smoking Jimmy's face. "Now you look, in order for you to rise to the top of the totem pole, you're going to have to get rid of a bunch of dangerous people. People from the old world that will slay you and everybody you care about for one false move. Do you understand what I am saying to you?"

Jimmy kicked his Jordan's up on the table and puffed on his Cuban cigar. "Look muthafucka, I just showed you what I think about the old world. I left three of the boss' dead with no regard. If you and I hadn't bumped heads a week in advance I woulda stanked yo' ass, too. The fact that you're still alive is a blessing within itself, a blessing that I've extended to you."

Mark wiped the sweat from his bald head. He wished he'd never gotten tangled up with the street animal. Now that he had he was desperate to find a way to get rid of him when the time was right. "Jimmy, I know what you've done for me. But after the mishap with Diego, you were also lookin' for another way to plug into the Island. The Marotta Family was your only in. If I had to guess, I'd say you made at least one million dollars in cash ever since our merger." He sat back in his seat and rubbed his hands together.

Jimmy laughed and blew a big cloud of smoke across the boardroom. "After you lay your killas, and cop new product, gas prices, travel arrangement, and tariffs to certain mafuckas that's navigating in the game that I must pay homage too in order to stay in bidness. Man, the value of a million dollars ain't shit. This is New York. A muthafucka needs millions and millions of dollars to survive. So, you ain't talking shit to the Capo, Dunn, word up."

This made Mark even more irritated. "Jimmy, I am Italian, a fuckin' Sicilian. I'm sorry if the men of my bloodline don't wanna jam with bloodthirsty blacks. That's just the way the game goes. That racist shit still exists, and unfortunately, I am just a small player in the grand scheme of it all."

Jimmy stood up and slammed his hand on the table so hard he cracked the wood. "I don't give a fuck what you saying, right now, Kid! Word to Janine! Yo, I saved yo muthafuckin' life, and I knocked off three of the boss' that were dead set on doublecrossing and exterminating the Marottas. Nigga you owe me. You owe me, or you're forcing my hand!" He took out two .40 Glocks and slammed them on the table with both barrels aimed at Mark. Then took a grenade out of his jacket and tossed it up and down in his hand.

Mark grew spooked. "Is that what I think it is?"

Jimmy mugged him. "Muthafucka, you just don't get it. I got Harlem on my back, Son. If I don't feed my trenches, then they don't eat. That's a lot of starving people. That shit ain't going go over well. Before I let my people starve, we'll be on some cannibalism type shit. Harlem a eat a Marotta every day, three times a day until you muthafuckas get it through your head that we run New York! My people can't starve! That shit ain't happening—period!"

Mark sat back in his seat and mugged Jimmy. He was at a loss for words. He scratched his bald head and sighed, "Okay, Jimmy, I have a deal for you, but it's going to take some whacking. We need to move some people in the family around. Once they are out of the picture, I move up another step. The farther upward I travel the better off for Harlem. So, have a seat and listen up. This is what I need."

Jimmy allowed himself to calm down. He took a seat at the long table and interlocked his fingers. "Spit that shit out and I'ma show you how me and mine get down for Uptown."

Chapter 12

Yasmin pulled the covers back from the pallet on the floor and stretched her arms above her head. She had a big smile on her face. The sun shined through the uncovered apartment window. She had yet to get some form of curtains to cover it, but she felt good, and so did the light shined directly on her. She looked over at a sleeping Bonkers. The covers were pulled down just enough to showcase his abs. She couldn't help but take her hand and slide it over them. The ripples felt so good to her.

She snuggled back up to him and kissed his cheek. "Good morning, baby."

Bonkers slowly opened his eyes. His stomach was growling worse than he could ever remember, and his morning erection hurt. He and Yasmin had been screwing all night for the second night in the row. Not only was he still tired, but he felt woozy and sick.

The heroin was calling him like an angry mother. "Yo', good morning to you too, Goddess."

Yasmin smiled harder. "Baby, I'm finna jump up and go cook us something to eat. I can hear your stomach growling like a Panther." She laughed and slid out of the pallet.

Bonkers yawned and sat up. He took a hold of his morning wood and squeezed it. He prayed it went down soon. His thing hurt so bad he didn't even wanna look at it. He grabbed his phone from the cushions on the couch and saw that he had more than one message from Kammron. Another from Jimmy telling him they all needed to have a sit-down. He'd been laid up with Yasmin and kicking it with Yazzy for an entire week straight.

He'd blown through thirty thousand dollars easily, and after placing the furniture order was set to blow through another fifteen. He saw right away that having a family costs some serious dough. Finally, his piece went down.

He stood up and stretched. "Yasmin, don't worry about the breakfast ma. I'm finna jump in this shower, kiss Yazzy a few times. Then I gotta hit Uptown and see what it do wit' the fellas. I done had a long enough vacation. Nah, mean?"

Yasmin frowned and came back into the living room. She stepped into his face. "God, you talking all this kissing, Yazzy stuff. What about me, though, don't I get some of those kisses?" She nuzzled her nose across his three times, before kissing his lips sensually. Her tongue danced with his as she wrapped her arms around his neck.

Bonkers couldn't help it, he had to grab that fat ass booty and squeeze the cheeks. It was one of Harlem's finest asses, he could vouch for that. Their kissing caused his piece to stiffen again.

He cursed under his breath and backed up. "Yo', word to Janine you gotta chill, Goddess. We smashed like ten times last night, and some this morning. My joint killing me!" He clutched it and gritted his teeth.

"Aww, poe baby," Yasmin teased. "You want me to kiss it?" She kneeled on one knee.

The sight only made him harder. "Nah shorty, get ya ass up. You only making by shit hurt worst. I'm about to go and hit this water. He walked out of the living room holding himself.

"Wait, Bonkers, I just wanna get one thing straight between us before you do. I'm not trying to get on ya mental a nothing, but I just need to know for myself."

He turned around. "What's good?"

She stepped back into his face and took a hold of his hands. "I just need to know if it's going to be me and you,

104

that's all?" She looked down to the floor, then trailed her eyes up to his.

Bonkers nodded his head. "Yo', I ain't perfect, we both know that. I definitely wanna do right by you, and Yazzy. So, in order for that to happen, yeah, it's gon' have to be me and you. I'm willing to fight for us if you are."

Yasmin nodded. "I am baby, I swear I am. I know it's not going to be easy, but I swear, I'm ready to fight for our family." She stepped into his embrace and hugged him tightly. "Let's just take it one day at a time, that's all we can do," she said, feeling her eyes water. The vision of her daughter having both her mother and father was enough to make her emotional.

Bonkers held her. "Yo', every child should have their moms and pops living under the same roof. Yazzy, is no different, we got this."

Those words were like music to Yasmin's ears. She looked up to Bonkers and shuddered. "God, is so good."

****

Kammron sat on the living room floor of Stacie's crib wiping down his guns with a rag dipped in alcohol. He had a big blunt in the corner of his mouth, and a focused look on his face. He was high and feeling real breezy.

Shelly stepped into the living room, and her eyes got big as paper plates. "Kamm, what the hell are you in here doing?" she wanted to know.

Kammron mugged her and took the blunt out of his mouth. "Fuck it look like? I gotta get my shits in order. I ain't about to having my toolies jamming up on me once I get to bucking these bitches." He oiled up the insides of each Glock, then switched over to the 45s. There was a total of twenty guns on the floor.

"Boy, if my mama comes in here and sees this, she gon' have a fit. Why you ain't do this shit at your new apartment?" she asked, stepping over a few pistols so she could sit on the couch across from him.

"Yo', mama already saw me, and besides I pay the rent up in this mafucka. If I wanna roll a tank through this bitch and oiled it up, before I wipe the interiors down wit' alcohol then I'll do just that. Only mafucka acting like they got a problem wit' it is you." His words cut more than he meant them too. He was just looking to give her a hard time as usual. Sometimes he liked to see her get all out of her body. "So, leave me the fuck alone with yo nosey ass."

Shelly frowned and hopped up. "Kamm, on Stacie, I'll buss ya fuckin' head. You ain't gon be talking to me like I'm one of these low life gutter snipes in Harlem. You gon' give me, my respect, nigga-fa real." She stood over him as if she were about to kick him in the chest or something.

Kammron laughed and continued to clean the Glock in his hand. "Shorty you better sit yo ass down and respect the God. This ain't what you think it is."

"Nigga, fuck you, I ain't scared of yo' ass. I sit around this mafucka all day long, humble, while you pop off at the jaw like I'm supposed to keep taking that shit. Nigga, please, I'm a muthafuckin woman, and I'll buss ya head if you don't respect me! Word up."

Kammron stood up with two guns in his hand. "Yo', who the fuck you talking to, shorty?" He stepped into her face just knowing she was going to back down.

Shelly looked up at him with her nostrils flared. "I'm talking to ya ass. You gon' respect me, Dunn. You won't the only one Harlem bred. I'm down fa mines, too."

"Oh, yeah?" Kammron pressed.

"Yeah, muthafucka."

Kammron took both Glocks and pressed them to each side of her temple. He cocked the hammers. "I'll blow ya lace front off ya head, shorty. You know my muthafuckin' name. This Killa, one-forty-fifth, and Lennox, thoroughbred. I'll knock them Ramens out ya head and won't think two shits about it. Now apologize, apologize or Stacie about to have one big mess to clean up."

Shelly trembled and swallowed her spit, as she felt the cold steel sitting on her temple. She imagined him blowing her brains out. Her dying at the age of nineteen-years-old. She'd just turned nineteen at that.

I have so much more life to live,' she thought. *'So much more life outside of Harlem.'* Then instead of relenting to his craziness, she became angry. "You know what, Kammron, fuck you, nigga! You gon' buss those guns you better make sure you take me out nigga or I'm coming for your ass. Ain't no hoes over here. Matter fact—" She pushed him as hard as she could, picked up a gun from the floor and aimed it at him. "—now what? Do what you gotta do."

Kammron scrunched his face. "Bitch, you ain't got the balls to squeeze that trigger. On everythang, you don't."

Shelly cocked the hammer and pulled the trigger over and over aiming at his feet, it clicked again and again. "Fuck you talking 'bout? Nigga ya lucky."

Kammron couldn't believe her courage. He rushed her, slammed her into the wall, dropped his guns, and ripped her dress from her body. Next was her panties, then he got his piece out, and picked her up.

She wrapped her legs around him and started fighting him off. "Get off of me, Kammron! Get off of me!"

Kammron found her opening and slid into her. He bounced her up and down on his dick, fucking her hard. "Huh-uh-uh-uh." He still couldn't believe that she'd had enough gall to pull those triggers. He was sure she didn't know if they were loaded or not. That excited him.

"Mmm-mmm, stop Killa, mmm! Aww-stop-stop-stop! Aww—shit, Killa!" She was hoisted up and down. She could feel his piece going deep into her body. She closed her eyes and began enjoying the pleasure.

Stacie came out of her bedroom and stopped in the middle of the hallway. Paralyzed by what Kammron was doing to her oldest daughter. She wanted to open her mouth to tell them to stop, but the scene left her speechless, and a bit intrigued. She clamped her thighs together and remained planted in place.

Kammron bounced her up and down on his dick. Her juices seeped out of her hole and spilled down his thighs. He fell to the floor with her. Threw her thighs on his shoulders, and really got to fuckin' her hard.

Shelly bit into her bottom lip and sucked on it to keep from moaning out loud. It felt so good! Whenever he took the pussy from her it was like it took her arousal to new heights. The brute of it all. The way his dick beat through her tunnel and hit her G-spot, again and again, was enough to drive her crazy.

"Mmm-mmm-mmm-mmm-mmm—oooo-mmm!" She felt her orgasm mounting. She squeezed her eyelids tight and turned her face to the left before opening them again. The sight of her mother scared the shit out of her, but it was too late, she was cumming hard. "Kammron—Kammm!" she hollered.

Kammron kept digging in that pussy. His back was like a snake. He sucked on her neck and rolled her slam home. Her heat drove him nuts. When he looked toward the hallway and saw Stacie with her hand between her thighs it was too much. They locked eyes, and she rushed back to her bedroom and closed the door. He came watching her ass jiggle in her nightgown.

****

Three hours later he rolled the Porsche while Bonkers sat in the passenger's seat nodding his head to a Hov track that was bumping out of the speakers.

"Yo, this nigga, Jimmy saying he got some biz for us, Kid. It's about time, too. Son, been in and out if the Apple all week every time I try and get a hold of him, he ain't been available." Kammron cruised with the top dropped. It was mid-August, and the weather was scorching.

Bonkers sipped a Tahitian Treat. "Yo, whatever he talking we need to see what it do. I ain't know having a family was this fuckin' expensive. Yo', it seems like every time I look up it's always something I gotta fit the bill for. I mean it ain't getting the best of me or nothin', but damn, it's most definitely different," he said thinking about how the furniture bill had just hit his pockets.

Kammron laughed. "Yo', ain't nobody tell you to wife Shorty. That's what the fuck you get. You coulda took care of, Yazzy, from a distance like every other nigga from Harlem, do their shorties."

"Yeah, well, I ain't every other, nigga. I gotta do right by, Yazzy, B. The only way I'm gon' be able to do that is if I hold her moms down like a man instead of a bitch. I know it's plenty pussy out here, but ain't none of them pussies pop out my seed, Killa. I owe shorty more than a lot."

Kammron nodded. "Yeah, I hear that, God. You gotta do what you gotta do. The family thing may be your route to go in life. But for the kid, yo' this where my focus is real heavy. Check out my new ropes, these joints got lemon diamonds in them. A hunnit gees a piece. The diamonds a quarter million. This Rolex ninety bands. These are my kids, B, word up. Later for that family shit. The God only a young nigga still." He laughed and punched the Porsche. Then blew his horn at two thick ass caramel chicks walking down Frederick Douglas Boulevard. They threw their arms up. He laughed again.

"Yo,' Killa, you make a nigga feel real bad for trying to do the right thing, Kid. I mean if you were in my shoes what would you do?" Bonkers asked looking over at him.

Killa continued to push his Porsche. "Yo, word to, Kathy, if a nigga seven feet tall, weighing in at five hundred pounds of solid muscle, I ain't scared, I'll fight his ass. Fuck nigga put a gun to my head and say he gon' pull the trigger, I ain't scared. I'm from Harlem, son, I live by the gun, I'ma die by the gun. You wanna know the only thing I'm scared of on God's green earth?"

Bonkers looked over at him. "What's that, Dunn?"

"Yo,' a bitch saying she missed her period." He was dead serious.

Bonkers busted up laughing. He slapped his thigh, and almost dropped the Mac-11 off of his lap. "Yo', my word, Kid I thought you was going to say somethin' else. The Feds, twelve, any mafuckin' body, and yo silly ass gon say a bitch missing her period." He was cracking up.

Kammron looked him over. "Word to, Kathy, B. That's it, now let's roll over here, and see what's good wit', Jimmy."

Chapter 13

Kammron stood holding the tray of small plates while adjusting his Tuxedo jacket. He felt the weight of the heavy knives and curled his lip. He looked around the huge Banquet hall and saw people walking around with little plates of food that he wouldn't eat even if a mafucka put a gun to his head. He didn't like rich people food. If he couldn't pronounce it, he wasn't eating it. He wanted to kick Jimmy's ass for having them pose as waiters to the crowd full of rich ass holes. All in the name of a mission.

Bonkers tried one of the small knishes and spit it back out. He took the plate, dumped it inside of the garbage can, picked his tray back up and shook his head. "Yo', fuck this shit, Dunn? This taste like drywall a somethin'." He popped a stick of Extra gum inside of his mouth and surveyed the room.

Jimmy had given them two marks to knock off. Bonkers picked his target. A tall Italian man with black, wavy hair, dressed sharply, with a cockiness to his demeanor. Bonkers watched the way the man interacted with the other people in the room. It was clear he was a man of power and substance. Bonkers didn't know him, but he didn't like him either.

Kammron walked over to him. "Yo,' Kid, I'm ready to sweat these spaghetti heads and keep it moving. Word is bond, I don't feel right serving 'em and shit."

An older white lady came up to Kammron and took one of the small plates off his tray. She looked him up and down and tilted her head toward the ceiling, before walking off.

Kammron had to catch himself from saying something stupid. "Yo', I see my lick headed toward the bathroom, Dunn. I'm finna go finish his ass so I can get the fuck out of here." He dumped the entire tray into the trash and followed behind the shorter, Italian, heavy-set man.

Bonkers watched them disappear down the hallway. He eyed his mark from across the room. The man picked up a champagne glass, grabbed the hand of a blond woman, twirled her in a circle, and placed his arm around her neck. His phone vibrated in his pocket. He took it out and saw a message from Yazzy, and Yasmin telling him they missed him. He smiled and replaced it. His mark moved toward the back of the banquet hall and rounded the corner. He slowly made his way in the direction of the man. Along the way, he'd stop and serve the occupants of the get-together. When he got to the hallway, he set the tray on the counter and crept down the long hallway.

****

Kammron locked the bathroom door and stepped up to the urinal beside his heavyset mark. He pretended like he was about to piss, looked over at the man and cheesed. "Ain't nothing like a nice long piss. Am I right?"

The mark frowned and turned his nose up at him. "You just make sure you wash your filthy hands before you go back out there and work. In fact, I'm going to make sure that you do." He gave him a look of disgust.

Kammron jerked his head back offended. "Aww, is that how we feeling today? What you think cause I'm out there serving guests that it makes you better than me a somethin'?"

The mark flushed the urinal and stepped up to the sink. "I'm a Marotta, I am better than you on every level." He turned off the sink and grabbed a hand towel to dry his hands. "Now get over here and wash your dirty hands or I'll be forced to call your superiors and tell them how disgusting you are. I'll recommend that you are fired immediately."

Kammron flushed the urinal and laughed. "Aww, you making this fun for me." He stepped over to the sink.

112

"I beg your pardon?" The mark asked.

Kammron pulled a knife from his jacket and grabbed him by the neck. "Muthafucka if you scream, I swear to God I'ma cut your throat out."

The mark wasn't trying to hear no parts of that. He swung and punched Kammron in the jaw then made a run for the door. Kammron shook his hit off immediately and pursued him. Before the man could reach the door, he slammed the knife into his back, pulled it out, and slammed it into him again. The mark fell to his knees in pain. Kammron stabbed him in the jaw as hard as he could with the knife. The blade ripped through his tender flesh and implanted itself in his mouth. The point was lodged in his tongue, blood spewed from his orifice right away. The mark tried his best to holler in pain, but his throat began to fill with the liquid of his blood.

Kammron drug him back to the middle of the bathroom and stood over him. "Talk that shit now, Money. Come on, I can't hear you, Kid. You need to put some base in your voice. He kneeled and started stabbing him in the face over and over again. As he slashed and slammed, blood popped up and rained on his clothes. "Punk muthafucka, now I got some shit to wash off my hands."

****

Bonkers waited until his mark stepped into the coat room before he rushed behind him and wrapped his arm around his neck. He tightened his grip, started choking him out and kicked the door closed, before slinging him to the floor.

The mark fell to his ass, his face was white with terror. "What's the meaning of this? I don't understand!" He scooted back on his ass. "I don't have any cash on me, but I can get you some if that's what you want."

Bonkers locked the door and pulled out his deer hunting knife. He pointed the blade at the man. "You're trying to stop Harlem from advancing by blocking the coke supply. Word on the street is that you got somethin' against my peeps."

The mark was confused. He didn't understand anything that came out of Bonkers' mouth. He felt he was being set up. He had to reason with the man. Yeah, that was the only way to go. "Hey, I swear, I don't know what you're talking about. But listen to me, I can make you a rich man. I'm talking filthy rich. If you give me the chance, I'll give you five million dollars. You'll never have to worry about anything again. All it'll take is one phone call. Please, let me make that call."

Bonkers smirked at him. "Nah, Kid, that ain't how his shit go. I have my orders." He rushed him, jumped on top of him, slammed the knife into his throat, and pressed on it with all of his might.

The mark kicked his legs in the air. He felt like he was being choked. The blade penetrated his windpipe. His eyes were open as wide as they could go. A lone tear trailed down his cheek. He tried to push Bonkers off of him.

Bonkers ripped the knife out of his throat and watched him struggle for his next breath. The sight amused him. "Wit' yo punk ass out the game, Harlem finna take this coke shit to the next level, homeboy. You can thank yo' nephew Mark for this." He raised the knife over his head and slammed it into his temple.

The mark felt the knife burrow through his cranium. The blade sliced a path into his brain and ripped the muscles and tissue there. Blood poured out of his nose, and down his throat. He blinked twice before his life left his body.

****

Later that night, Jimmy threw a small get together in the VIP private room section of Club Diamonds for himself, Bonkers, and Kammron. He purchased five bottles of Ace of Spades and handed Kammron, and Bonkers two bottles a piece, before setting up ounces of Tar on the table.

Kammron popped both bottles and drank from one at a time. "This how you do that, boss shit. Fuck saving one for later. I drink these hoes just like this." He took turns swallowing from each bottle. "Where the bitches at, Kid?"

Jimmy sat in the middle of the booth. "Oh, we finna do the damn thing, but not yet. First of all, this is for y'all." He picked up a duffel bag from the floor, sat it on his lap, unzipped it and pulled out fifty thousand dollars in cash. "Huh, Bonkers, this is just an advance for the next job. I might need you today, or maybe even tomorrow. Shid, I might not need you until next year, but it don't matter. I wanna get it to where every time I rub elbows with you li'l niggas I'm hitting y'all wit' a heavy lump sum."

"Fuck mine at then, god? The Kid definitely trying to eat, big boy status too," Kammron said, rubbernecking into the duffle bag.

Jimmy laughed. "Yo', you know the Capo can't forget about you, Killa. Word up, however, my li'l brother eating that's how you gon be eating, too. We all in this shit together." He pulled out fifty more thousand in rubber-banded money and handed it to Kammron.

Kammron set his bottles on the table and took a hold of the cash. "Yo, how much scratch is this?"

"Fifty gees, a piece that is. Y'all been one hunnit since day one. You two li'l niggas do the work of an army. I admire that," Jimmy admitted.

"Say, Dunn, when you gon' miss us wit' all that lil nigga talk?" Kammron asked stuffing his pockets with his newly received cash.

"Yeah, Jimmy, lil niggas don't get down like we do. We more like big niggas, Kid. Word to Janine." Bonkers was filling his pockets with his cash as well.

"Yo, before I answer that question, I got one of my own. Are y'all ready to get ya hands on some serious life-altering chips?" Jimmy looked from Bonkers to Kammron.

Kammron filled the inside of his Marc Jacobs jacket with twenty thousand. "Yo', you already know we fiending for the dough. What you want done, B. My word, if it's got a fifty-thousand-dollar price tag on it consider that shit done."

Jimmy shook his head. "That's peanuts to the Capo. I'm talkin' some serious chips. Hunnits of thousands at a time. Some shit you can really move and groove with."

"Yo', spit that shit out, big bruh. You got our attention." Bonkers grabbed a bottle of his champagne and sipped from it. He couldn't get Yazzy off his mind. The fifty thousand could help him do a lot for her, and Yasmin.

"I know you niggas love this killing shit. I know it's addicting, but I want y'all to be a jack of all trades when it comes to the game. I'm trying to bring back the forgotten trade to Harlem. Coke."

Kammron frowned and looked to Bonkers. "Yo', mafuckas in Harlem don't be wilding over that white like they do that dog food, B. If we trying to make some serious paper it gotta be that tar shit."

Jimmy shook his head. "That's where you're wrong, Killa. Not only is it, crazy cash still in coke, but it's what's going to get us filthy rich. Trust me on this, we ain't gon' be on no nickel and dime type shit. I'm talking birdies. Fifty at a time from coast to coast. The Capo got a plug that's gon' help us do some crazy numbers. Only thing is, you Gods gon' have to travel a lil bit. All of the new cities we break into we're going to be looking to take over operations that are already flourishing. In order for us to penetrate those circles, we're going to take the heads right off their bosses and set up shop. It's cutthroat, it's conniving, it's selfish, it's—"

"It's Harlem, son!" Kammron held up two bottles and drank from both of them at the same time. "Yo', I'm down like Brandy Norwood."

Bonkers rubbed his chin. "You gon' already have the moves set in place or what?"

"Most definitely, you know how I do. The more places we take over the bigger our profits. First, outta state venture, I'm sending you niggas too is Ohio. Columbus, Cincinnati, Cleveland, and Youngstown."

Kammron laid back on the couch. "Nigga, you set it up, and me and the Homie a show and prove. Yo', but ex that lil nigga shit, though. Mafuckas ain't shorties no more. Honor us as Gods, word up."

Bonkers ran his blade through a small like of Tar. Made him two lines and took one to the head. He smacked his lips as the high took over him right away. "Yo', I agree with, Killa Kamm. I don't like hearing that li'l nigga shit. We ain't gotta prove to you how big we are. Respect the Gods, Son. Word to Janine."

Jimmy nodded his head. "Slim that's the least I can do. It's all love, besides I'm finna make you Gods heavyweights. That's on everything."

Kammron stood up with both bottles. "Yo', I got a thousand in ones. Let's say we call them bitches in here and get it in. I need something thick in my lap."

Jimmy stood up and gave him half of hug. "Bruh, I know we ain't always seen eye to eye, but my word, I got a lot of respect for you. I just want to let you know that there are no hard feelings. It's all love over this way, Dunn."

Kammron sat his bottles down and gave him half of hug. "Feelings are for bitches, nigga, and so are grudges. It's good over here, Jimmy, word to my moms. You just follow up your words with actions. Get me and my man's chips all the way up like Vegas, and you a see the loyalty bust out a nigga like you been seeing." He hugged him tight.

Kammron turned to Bonkers. "Yo', get ya ass up, Bonkers. I know you got Yazzy dominating ya mental, but you with the fellas, right now. We need to know we're all on the same page and we trust each other. I mean I know you trust, Killa, but I need to know that you trust me, too. After all, we're all the family that we have."

Bonkers stood up and hugged Kammron. "You know it's all love, God. I trust you to the fullest."

Kammron hugged him back and nodded. "That goes without saying." He stepped back.

Bonkers stepped up to Jimmy. "Yo', you're my, big brother. We bleed the same blood, Kid. Came out of the same womb. Yo', it's for me to think that you got my best interest at heart. I mean the fight between us is still in the back of my mind, but it's still money over everythang. I'm down wit' you, Jimmy, one hunnit percent." He hugged him and held the back of his head.

"A mafucka ain't studding that fight. Losses happen to the best of us. It is what it is. You won't win all of em, just like I won't." He stood back. "Let's just focus on the money now. Agreed?"

"Agreed."

Chapter 14

Kammron stepped up the stairs of the stoop tipsy. He staggered a few feet after making it on the porch and slid his key into the lock of his new apartment when Stacie blew the horn of her Plymouth Neon. He turned around and shielded his eyes from the street lights.

Stacie threw her car in park and jumped out of it. She walked up the steps to his stoop. "Boy, I been hitting yo' ass up all night. Why you ain't respond to none of my texts?" She asked sizing him up.

Kammron licked his lips. He looked Stacie from head to toe. Her thick thighs were damn near busting through her Capris. "Yo', what you tracking me down for?" He asked, feeling some type of way. He turned, pushed open the door, and made his way up the stairs that led to his front door.

Stacie closed the main door behind her and followed him up the stairs. It's not that I was trying to track you down, but we definitely have to talk." She stopped behind him and waited until he stepped inside his crib.

Kammron opened the door, strolled to his couch, took a seat, and flipped on Sports Center. He began to check the NBA scores on the bottom of the screen. He wanted to see what type of numbers Zion Williamson was putting up.

Stacie locked the door, kicked her shoes off, and made her way across the carpet. She was five-feet-two-inches tall, brown-skinned, with brown eyes, and the body of a Harlem Goddess. At forty years old she could give any bitch in the hood a run for their money. She sat on the couch and crossed her thick thighs. She didn't know how to say what she was about too. She knew Kammron had a quick temper, and that he got mad at the drop of a hat. But she felt certain things needed to be said and understood.

She took a deep breath and exhaled slowly. "Kammron, how long have you and I, known each other?"

Kammron continued to watch the NBA highlights. "Yo', the God been knowing you ever since I was ten years old. Why what's good?"

"And in that amount of time, I've always tried my best to keep it real with you. I've done all that I could to help you when things got rough and stuff, right?"

He nodded. "And in exchange, I made sure that I tackled all of your bills on time, and in advance most of the times so you said all of that to say what?"

Stacie felt a strike of anger. "A'ight, you have, but this ain't about that."

Kammron flicked off the television and looked her over. "A'ight ma, then what it's about?" His eyes trailed over her thick thighs. He could see the underside of her voluptuous ass. It looked so good to him, he felt his penis stir. Stacie had always given him mommy issues.

"Boy, I'm just gon' come right out and say it. Shana's ass is two months pregnant, and she's saying you are the father."

Kammron hopped up taken aback. "What?"

Stacie nodded her head, her lace front curls bounced on her shoulders. "Yep, I didn't know what to say to that because the last I checked you was supposed to be rocking with, Shelly. So, what's really up with you? Are you fuckin' my youngest daughter, too?"

Kammron ran his hand over his head. "Yo', you gotta be fuckin' kidding me, Stacie. Shorty can't be pregnant. Not by me anyway."

"That ain't answering my question, Kammron. Are you fuckin' my baby or not?"

Kammron brushed his waves with his brush. He looked at the floor for a long time. "Yo', I wax that ass a few times, but it wasn't nothing serious. She got a nice shot on her, but I ain't on no baby mama shit. Yo', we gotta sit down and talk like a-sap. Word to Kathy."

Stacie was in disbelief. She stepped forward and smacked him. "You son of a bitch! How could you do that to me? I trusted you around, Shana, and this is what you do?"

Kammron held his face and mugged her. "Yo', I understand you mad and all, but I'ma need you to keep your hands to yourself. You acting like Shana innocent in all of this. You should have seen how she kept throwing the pussy at a nigga. She mighta been young but she was most definitely ready." He snickered.

Stacie's eyes got bucked she reached to swing her right hand again, but he caught her wrist. "Let me go, Kammron! This is some bullshit, and you know it. I gotta get the fuck out of here." She broke away from him and rushed toward the front of the door, vexed.

Kammron smashed her stomach against the front door. He humped forward into her ass, felt the cushions of it, and moaned deep within his throat "What you finna do, huh?" More grinding into her backside.

Stacie closed her eyes. "Get off me, Kamm, I can't even believe you, right now."

He held her hips and worked his front into her. "I've always had a thing for you, Stacie. You're a sexy ass mother. Badder than both of your daughters. That's a fact. You gave a young nigga all types of issues the way you used to walk around the house." He reached under her clothes and took a hold of her breasts.

She hated the forbidden feeling that went through her. "Get off me, Kamm, stop playin' wit' me." She gasped and sounded out of breath.

Kammron sucked on the back of her neck and kept her molded to the front door. His tongue traced up and down her skin, before he bit into her with his teeth, and sucked hard.

She shivered. "Kammron, honey, please! Let me go, you know this ain't right," she whispered out of breath.

Kammron flipped her around and made her raise her hands over her head. Their fingers interlocked. He kissed her lips, licked them and sucked on her bottom one. Then he was all over her neck, pulling her to him.

Stacie moaned. "Baby, please son, don't! Unnhhh—" She couldn't deny that her nipples were hard. That her panties were wet.

Over the years there had been a few tikes that caused crazy sexual thoughts to come into her mind in regards to Kammron, but she'd tried her best to wipe her mind clear of them. She'd known him since he was a little boy. In her mind, he was like her son. So, it felt weird when his hands traveled under her sweater and unhooked her bra in the front. Then he was squeezing her soft breasts and pinching the nipples. She moaned louder.

Kammron kissed her lips again. "Let's worry about that other shit later, Stacie. Tonight, it's just about you and your, baby boy. I promise we gon' handle that other stuff tomorrow." He raised her shirt and licked both of her dark brown nipples.

They were erect and looked so pretty to him. He remembered seeing their indentations poking through so many of her shirts. Stacie was a fox, he had to admit that. She pushed him away and jogged into the living room. She was trying to figure out what her next move should be. She knew it woulda been so wrong to screw her daughter's man. Especially after she'd practically raised him. It didn't matter how bad he had her middle tingling.

Kammron pulled his Polo shirt over his head and dropped it to the floor. Next came his black tank-top. "Stacie, look at this body. Look at The Kid, Shorty, and tell me you ain't feeling the God." He ran his hand over his abs. There was an imprint from his piece sticking up against his Polo shorts.

Stacie sucked her bottom lip into her mouth. She felt like she was getting ready to panic. "Look, Kammron, I ain't on that. I got more respect for myself, and more love for my daughters than that. Now, I'm finna go. You need to drop by the house tomorrow so we can talk about this li'l situation with, Shana. Okay?" She fixed her D cup breasts back into their cups. Her nipples were so hard they were killing her.

Kammron lowered his head. "Yo', you know what mama, I'm bogus for even coming at you like that. Yo', for as long as you been in my life you ain't been nothing but a blessing. I got more respect for you than I been showing." He picked up her shoes and held them out to her.

Stacie breathed a sigh of relief. "Thank you for saying that, baby, I really mean that." She grabbed her shoes from him and put them on one by one. When she was dressed appropriately and ready to go. She stepped to the front door. Kammron stood on the side of it with his head down. This made her feel some type of way. "Honey, it's okay, I'm not mad at you. A'ight?" She stepped in and hugged his frame. "Mama, still love you, boy."

The scent of her perfume sent sexual waves up his nose. He hugged her tighter and slid his hands down to her fat ass. "Ma, I'm sorry, I gotta have some of you tonight. I'll suffer the consequences tomorrow." He snatched her up into his arms and carried her to his bedroom, ignoring the fight she was putting up.

He tossed her on the bed, got between her thighs, pushed her sweater above her breasts, and yanked the bra back open, ripping a portion of the material in the process. Her titties spilled out. He cupped them, pushed them together and sucked on the hard nipple, pulling them from their mounds, while he grinded between her thighs.

"Unnhhh, Kammron, stop baby. Don't do me like this," he uttered faintly and made a mock attempt to push him off of her.

Kammron rubbed her pussy through her jeans. He could feel her heat. His fingers reached all the way down to her ass crack. Then he was unbuttoning them and pulling them off her thighs. He flung the Capris against the wall, slipped his hand into her panties, and felt her trimmed cat. The heat from her cave was arousing. Her lips were covered with dew. She was wet, there was no ignoring that fact.

"Uhhh, please, baby." She felt his middle finger penetrate her opening. Her thighs shot wide open, her back arched. Then he had two of his digits running in and out of her body. Before she could control her movements, she found herself humping his hand with reckless abandon. "Uh-uh-uh-uh, baby, baby— stop!"

Kammron finger fucked her faster and faster, while he worked his shorts off. His dick sprung through his boxer hole. He yanked them off and got between her legs. He rubbed his dick up and down her center, then angled it downward, and slipped into her warmth.

As soon as Stacie felt him invade her crease she came, screaming as loud as she could. Her thighs wrapped around his waist. She pulled him down to her and licked his lips.

"I hate you for this, Kammron. I hate you! You so wrong, you so wrong, baby." She bucked her hips to consume more of him.

Kammron felt her grip and didn't give a fuck what she was talking about. He began fucking her as hard as he could,

124

remembering all the times she'd walked around him wearing next to nothing. That fat ass booty swallowing her panties. Her ass jiggling. He could always see her pussy lips from the back. She was built for sex. He loved growing up in her household. He sucked her neck loudly, threw her ankles on his shoulders, and drove in and out of her box.

"I knew it, I knew it, I knew it! Aahh, fuck, I knew it. This pussy so good. It's so good, mama! Give me this shit," he growled long stroking her pussy while he watched his dick go in and out of it.

Stacie shook and laid her head back on the bed. Another orgasm rocked her body as his dick rammed her. She couldn't believe how thick it was. How long he stretched inside of her. Every pump was an attack on her G spot. She squeezed his ass, and squirt all over his penis.

Kammron pulled out and flipped her over. "I gotta hit it from the back Stacie. Give me this shit!" He slid back in and proceeded to pound her out while he held her shoulders. He sucked his thumb into his mouth and slid it into her backdoor.

She yelped, only adding to his pleasure. Stacie pushed backward harder, and faster. She milked him with her insides and worked her pussy muscles as only a vet could. Every massage of her vaginal muscles sent shivers through his.

"Uhh, fuck me, Kammron. Uhhh, you're finally fuckin' me, baby!" She came again.

Kammron felt her squirt and that was all she wrote. He came in huge globs all in her pussy. He jerked into her ass. She fell on her stomach with his dick lodged deep within her, throbbing and pumping out his seed.

****

Stacie awoke early the next morning. She climbed out of his bed and stood over him. She stared at him for a long time, before she pushed his shoulder to wake him up. "Kammron, son wake up."

Kammron's eyes opened. He stretched his arms above his head. "Yo', good morning, sexy lady. How you doing?" He smiled and looked over at her. The sun shined through the window of his bedroom. He felt good, he could still smell the scent of their lovemaking in the air.

Stacie took a step closer and sat on the bed by his ribs. "Baby, you know what we did last night wasn't right. I slipped up and allowed your charming ass to get the better of me. I hate myself for it."

Kammron stretched his toes until his ankles popped. "Aww ma, you shouldn't be so hard on yourself. What's done is done."

She slapped him on the chest. "Boy, stop playin' wit' me. You know damn well that it was your fault more than it was mine. But anyway, you better take that to the grave with you. I'm serious, Kamm, my daughters can never find out what we did. That would destroy me."

Kammron sat up. "Yo', you know I can keep a secret better than, Victoria. They'll never know what we doing." He rubbed her thick thigh and nuzzled her neck.

"Not *doing* son—did." She pushed him off of her.

He grabbed her and pulled her down on the bed, then straddled her waist. "Yo', you talking about it as if we ain't gon do it a somethin'. You already know I got a taste of this body now I'm about to be fiending for it in a regular, so I gotta have it." He leaned down and kissed her neck.

Stacie held him back with both hands. "Boy, if you don't get yo ass up off me we gon' have a problem." She pushed him as hard as she could and stood up to fix her clothes. "Now, you need to get yo ass over to the house today so we can figure out this baby situation between. you and Shana. Far as Shelly go, pretty soon y'all gon' need to tell her what the deal is. It ain't fair for y'all to be going behind her back and doing what you did. I know I shouldn't be one to talk, but I am, so there." She opened the bedroom door. "Get yo' butt up, I'll see you later. It's time to man up, Kammron."

His last sights of her was watching her ass jiggle in her jeans, before she stepped into the hallway, and closed the door. He lowered his head. The Shana situation had him so irritated. He sat there for ten minutes stuck. He couldn't believe he'd slipped up the way he did. He jumped out of the bed, and before he made it to the bedroom door there was a loud pounding on his front door.

Chapter 15

Kammron looked through the peephole with a Glock .40 in his hand. He saw the face of an angry Shelly. He closed his eyes and he took a deep breath. He was sure Shelly had seen Stacie leave his building, and now she was set to demand answers. It was too early in the morning for so much drama.

He didn't feel like putting up with it. "Yo', what's good, Shelly?"

She frowned at the peephole. "*What's good?* Boy open the damn door and quit playing wit' me. I need to talk to you, like now!" she hollered.

Kammron shook his head. "What is it pertaining, too?"

Shelly beat on the door with both fists over and over again. "Open the damn door! Open the damn door, Kammron. Stop playin wit' me. Open the muthafuckin' door!" she screamed. Her heart thumped loudly in her chest.

Kammron opened the door and stood to the side. "Come on in, Goddess."

"Don't *Goddess* me, nigga. Yo', what's this shit about you getting my li'l sister pregnant?" She asked with her finger pointed at this temple.

Kammron slapped her fingers from his face. "Yo', get ya digits out my face and let me close this door. I don't need our business all in the street. This a new apartment. Did you forget?" He closed the doors and locked both locks.

Shelly was in his face again. "Son, when did you start fuckin' her li'l ass, huh? And, how could you? That's my muthafuckin' sister!" She was so heated she wanted to run the gun from him and empty the magazine in his forehead.

Kammron stepped past her. "Yo', that pregnant shit is bananas. She ain't pregnant by me. Shorty just thinks she got some kind of crush on me. Now she blowing it all out of proportion and shit. You know how the game go?"

Shelly smacked him as hard as she could, nearly dazing him. "Nigga, stop lying to me. I'm tired of you treating me like I'm one of them stupid bitches uptown. Yo', I got mad smarts, and I'm not some fluzzie. I'm not gon' let you treat me like one either. I been loyal to ya ass since we been together, and you gon' go behind my back and fuck my sister? Kid, I swear if I had a gun, I'd lace yo ass."

Kammron touched the crack of his mouth and looked at his fingers. There was blood. He cleaned it up with his tongue, swallowed, picked his head up and smiled at Shelly. "Shorty, this the last time I'ma ask you to keep yo muthafuckin' hands to yourself. I can understand you're mad and all that shit, but yo holler at me without your hands."

Shelly smacked her lips. "Fuck that, Killa! You got my sister pregnant. Is that not registering inside of this thick ass skull?" She poked at his forehead with her freshly manicured nails. "Yo', that's like me getting ready to have a baby by, Bonkers. How would you feel, Kid, huh? How would you feel if you found out ya nigga been stretching me out and spitting his seed all up in my treasures and shit? You'd be ready to kill my ass, right?" She stepped closer into his face. "*Right*?"

Kammron pushed her back. "Get the fuck out of my face! That's your last warning."

Shelly stumbled backward and caught her footing. She tried to get a hold of herself. "Just tell me why, Kamm? What would make you fuck her? What did I do wrong?"

Kammron ran his hand over his waves. "Yo', it ain't got shit to do wit' you, Goddess. Ya sister all thick and shit. She been in the picture just as long as you have. I mean not on the same shit we on, but yo I had urges for her li'l ass too. So, I smashed, it ain't nothing serious, no feelings a nothing, and I

130

ain't do it to yak at you. My word I just wanted to fuck. That's just what it was. Now she hollering this pregnant shit, and I fucked up, Goddess. That's all there is to it."

Shelly felt the tears roll down her face. They were tears of a weak person. They were tears of a woman that was close to releasing a man indefinitely. "Yo', so after all, I've done to stand by ya ass none of that kept you from just wanting to smash my sister? I kicked down thirteen months when I was just sixteen years old faithfully. While you did your time in Juvie, and this is the thanks I get?" She closed her eyes as more tears sailed down her cheeks.

Kammron placed his gun in the small of his back. He felt like shit. He remembered she'd written him a letter every single day and sent pictures. She'd been working at McDonald's, every other Friday she sent him a hundred dollars. She had him living like a king on the inside. In that time, she was the only one that stood by his side. He was even able to reach out for Bonkers because Bonkers was serving the same thirteen-month stent. Damn, he felt worse than shit when he thought about things.

"Yo', I'm sorry, Shelly. On my mother I am. I swear I didn't think about things. I was simply on some carnal shit. I'm sorry. Just tell me what I gotta do for your forgiveness, and I'll do it."

"You got my sister pregnant, Kammron. She's having *your* kid soon. There is nothing you can do that will make things right. You've officially shattered me," she said this with her voice breaking. "There is no more love in this house of my heart for you." Now her tears were coming full fledge. She turned her back to him and covered her face.

Kammron lowered his head. "Damn, Shelly, I—"

She shook her head. "I gave you my all, Kammron. I mean I know I couldn't offer you the world before, I'm still trying to get my own life in order, but all that I had I set before you since I was a little girl. I would have never done to you, what you did to me. They say there is a thin line between love and hate. I never understood that saying until now. Kammron, I swear I hate you." She turned and bumped him as she walked past him. "You wanna know how you can pay me back for doing what you did to, my sister?"

"Yeah, I'll do anything, just tell me."

"You can do right by her. Y'all are having a baby. Make sure you man up and be there for her. Take care of your seed. Treat my sister like a Queen. A real man would make her a wife before she becomes a baby mother, for you I know that's a long reach, but at the very least just be one hunnit to her. That's all I ask, you do this, and I'll forgive you."

Kammron jerked his head back. "What? Nah, shorty I ain't tryna to be with your sister. I'm in love with you. I've always been in love with you."

Shelly stepped into his face. "Don't give me that bullshit, Kammron—just don't! There's no way you could be in love with me and be able to fuck, my sister. Killa, you are too far gone in these streets. You don't have a clue what love or being in love truly is. If you did you woulda never taken me through all of the things you have. You ain't in love with me or nobody else. You're in love with yourself."

Kammron took the shot and felt it wound him internally. "Yo', that's how you feel, Shorty?" He stepped into her face. "You think I'm in love wit' me, right?"

"Yep, yep, I sho the fuck do." She stood her ground and walked into his face.

Kammron couldn't take it anymore. The psycho bell went off in his head. He picked her up and carried her to the room as she started beating on his back for him to put her down. He dropped her to the bed and slammed the bedroom door.

132

"I'ma show ya ass how so in love with me I am." He rushed to the dresser and pulled out the .357. He opened the cylinder to make sure there was a bullet present and spun the chamber three times. He placed the barrel to his temple.

Shelly hopped up. "Kammron, what the hell are you doing?"

Kammron pulled the trigger twice. *Click! Click!* "I'm so in love with myself, right. I love me, right." He spun the cylinder again. "This how much I love myself, Shelly—this how much." He put the barrel to his temple and pulled the trigger three quick times. *Click! Click! Click!*

Shelly was about to go out of her mind with hysteria. "Kammron, please!"

"N'all, y'all don't get it. Y'all don't know what I'm going through. All y'all see is this outside, shit. Mafuckas don't know I'm really struggling—*I'm struggling!*" He spun the cylinder again and pulled the trigger three quick times. A tear fell down his cheek.

Shelly rushed over to him and tried to take the gun. "Give me this, baby. Give it, please! I'm begging you, Kammron."

He backed all the way up and held the gun to his temple. His vision was hazy. Her voice seemed as if it was echoing. He felt sick on the stomach. He sunk to the floor and dropped the gun. It thumped on the floor. His knees came to his chest. His eyes were bucked wide open.

Shelly slowly made her way over to him. She was shocked. She didn't know what had happened. She had never seen him in such a state of mind. She got down on her knees, shuffled across the carpet and took his face against her breasts. "Baby what's going on with you?"

Kammron's eyes continued to be bucked wide open. "Yo', I'm sorry, Shelly. I fucked up, ma, the God fucked up. I shoulda never did what I did to offend you. Yo', you're worth more than a shot of pussy. You been here since the beginning, Goddess. I been on some straight fuck shit, and it ain't fair." He squeezed his eyelids together. His depression kicked in full-fledged and began to get the best of him. Everything that he'd done wrong to cross Shelly began to play itself before his mind's eye. Every vision made him feel sicker and sicker.

Shelly pulled him over her lap and rubbed the side of his face. "It's okay, baby, we all do wrong. I am not without sin. I can't cast no stones at you, Kammron. You are clearly going through something, and you just need a shoulder to lean on, right now. I can be that shoulder, I got you."

He shook his head. "I fucked up, Shelly. I don't need no shoulder. I need you, I love you, ma. I need you to give me a chance so I can make things right."

She shook her head. "I can't Kammron, I just can't. But we don't need to focus on that, right now. What's important is that you get past this fight you are going through. I'll hold your hand, baby, I got you."

Kammron jumped back out of her embrace and stood up. "I don't need your sympathy, Shelly. Get the fuck out of my house ma."

She climbed to her feet. "Kamm, what's the matter? I just want to help you."

"Get the fuck out of my house, right now. You don't wanna be wit' me. Then leave, I don't give a fuck no more! It's plenty of bad bitches in this world. You ain't the only one." He wiped the tears from his face.

Shelly took a step toward him. "Kammron, something is not right with you. You need to talk to me, damn that other stuff."

"Fuck you, Shelly." His vision was so hazy he couldn't see straight. He wobbled back and forth. "You don't give a fuck about me." He pointed toward the door. "Get the fuck out. Get out now, bitch or I swear to God I'ma kill yo ass."

"Kammron, please baby, just talk to me. I'm here for you." She stepped up to him with her arms wide open. "I'm here for you."

He shook his head, then grabbed her by the throat and proceeded to choke her as hard as he could. "You wanna leave me. You don't understand what I'm going through. You don't get it!" He hollered choking her harder and harder.

Shelly hit at his hands. Her eyes rolled into the back of her head. Her air supply was cut all the way off. She struggled against him, terrified for her life. She grabbed at his shirt and ripped it. Then her nails were digging into his shoulders.

Kammron cried. "You hate me, Shelly! You hate me, I know you do. I can see it in your eyes." He squeezed with all his might.

Her neck cracked. She fell to her knees still swatting at his hands. Her lungs felt like they were close to exploding. Her heart was beating faster and faster. She took a deep breath and was unable to blow it back out. Her vision became as hazy he was. The room went from bright to an eerie shade of darkness. She felt weak. Her fight slowly dissipated from her. Her arms fell at her sides as he choked and choked her. When her lungs burst and her heart came to a standstill. He choked her for five more minutes and slung her to the floor.

He jumped up and paced back and forth looking down at her body. "I'm so sorry, Shelly, I'm so sorry!"

T.J. Edwards

Chapter 16

Bonkers stepped through Kammron's doorway four hours later. Kammron met him with a bottle of Patron in his hand. "Yo, you wouldn't tell me why you was calling me over here. All you kept saying was it was an emergency. Well, I'm here now. What's really good?"

Kammron locked the door, kept his silence, and waved for Bonkers to follow him as he led him to the back room. Kammron opened the door and stood to the side.

Bonkers looked Kammron over closely as he peeked his head inside the room. His eyes got bucked. "Yo, who the fuck is that under the sheet, Kid?"

Kammron turned up the bottle of Patron and walked away. He stumbled down the hall, taking long swallows from the liquor. When he got to the living room, he took a seat on the sofa and lowered his head.

Bonkers kneeled and pulled the sheet from over Shelly's face. "Aww, shit!" He jumped up. "What the fuck happened to her, Killa?" He peered down at her. Kammron had left her eyes wide open. Her pupils had turned bluish gray. Bonkers kneeled down and closed them. "Kammron, what the fuck, Kid?" He covered her back with the sheet and ran down the hallway. "What did you do, bruh? What the fuck did you do?"

Kammron took a swallow from the bottle. "I fucked, Stacie last night. She got some of the best pussy I've ever had in my entire life. After lusting after her for so many years, it felt good to finally get the pussy." He turned the bottle back up.

Bonkers frowned. "Yo, so what Shelly catch y'all in the mix, and came at you reckless? So, you had to put her down or something?"

"Shana talking about she pregnant now, too. I don't know if the baby mine or not, but I promised, Shelly, I would do right by her. So, I am." He belched and closed his eyes.

Bonkers sat on the couch and looked over at Kammron. "Nigga, what the fuck happened to her? What made you kill her?"

"Yo, she was talking about leaving me, Dunn. I can't see her with no other nigga. I was on some straight sucka shit, but it's too late to think about that, right now. She gone, bruh, I fucked up. I just wanted to show you what I did because I don't know where to go from here."

Bonkers was taken aback. None of what Kammron was saying made sense to him. He wanted to pry further but knew the more he pushed him the worst off he would be. He felt it was in his best interest to help him get rid of Shelly's body so they could move forward. "Say, Kid, I don't know what you goin' through, but I need you to know you're not alone. You fucked up, but I got you. We're in this shit together, always have been."

Kammron took a long swallow from the bottle. "I ain't never wanted to punch my lights out more than I want to do it, right now." He set the bottle on the table and stood up. "I just kilt the love of my life, Bonkers. What the fuck am I gon' do now?" He held out his arms.

Bunkers hopped up and hugged him. "Yo, it's your mental illness, Kid, it ain't ya fault. No matter what I ain't gon' leave you alone. We gon' handle this shit together."

****

Beep! Beep! Beep! Beep!

It was eleven o'clock at night, in late August, as Jimmy directed the U-Haul backward to the facility. When the truck backed up just enough so the cargo could be unloaded, he came around to the driver's side and tapped on the door. "Open this mafucka, Dunn, and let's pull these crates out." Jimmy jumped up on the dock of The warehouse and stood back as three of his men from Harlem pulled crates of can goods that were loaded with pure tar, and Peruvian flake.

Each can good that was labeled as string beans were really Vietnamese tar, and the ones labeled cream of corn was Peruvian flake. He rubbed his hands together as he imagined his profits. He was about to set the city on fire.

Mark Maratta placed his hand on his shoulder as he watched Jimmy's men load up the warehouse they would use as a distributing post. "I told you, Jimmy, if you remained loyal to me, I would make sure you'd wind up a very rich man. This is only the beginning. As a show of good faith, I'll need those three in Columbus taken care of immediately."

Jimmy looked him over from the corners of his eye. "Yo', a deal is a deal. I got Hittas already on it. You just fall back and let me orchestrate this shit. You dig that?"

Mark adjusted his suit coat. "Yeah, I can dig that, Jimmy."

****

Kammron took a step back and watched the flames that burned Shelly's body to nothing but bones. Bonkers stepped up to the big metal garbage can that they had struggled to push inside of the abandoned warehouse and poured more gasoline into the fire. The flames shot twenty feet high. The heat from the blaze was enough to cause both men to sweat along the foreheads.

Kammron shook his head. "Yo', I fucked up, Bonkers. I don't know what I was thinking, but I know without a shadow of a doubt that ain't nobody gon' love me as much as she did." He shielded his eyes from the brightness of the flames.

Bonkers came and stood beside him. "Bruh, what's done is done. We can't dwell on this mistake. I think you need to be dying to figure out what you're going to tell her peoples after she been missing for a long time. That's gon' be the hardest thing to do. How did she get over to your crib in the first place?"

"The subway, that's how she traveled period. Why?" Kammron wanted to know.

"Damn, that means cameras can track her every movement, and they gon' be able to tell what platform she got off on. The most they can do though is track her to your area. That don't mean she actually made it to your crib, but you gon' have to play the fool. Like, hit Shana, or Stacie about Shelly's whereabouts. You gotta make it seem like you been looking for her. Fuck wit' her social media, too. Run the whole gambit, nah mean?"

Kammron could smell the burnt flesh drift into the air. The scent made him sick on the stomach. "Yeah, I know what you mean, bruh." He downed the rest of his Tequila and drop broke the bottle on the ground. The flames danced before his eyes. "Yo, after we discard those bones and shit, I need you to take me to my Pop's crib."

"What—why you wanna go there all the sudden?" Bonkers inquired.

The last time Kammron visited his old man, he'd played two entire hours of Russian Roulette afterward. There was something about his father that bothered him. Something about the old man that set Kammron off.

"Yo, I just need to see him. There is some shit going on inside of me that I can't explain. Yo', I hate going to the fucking nut house, too Bonkers, and you ain't gotta go wit' me. I need to holler at him alone anyway. Just drop me off, Kid, and I'll spend the night wit' him. I'm begging you, bruh."

Bonkers nodded. "Yo', I got you, Dunn, but you know how the game go? If you needed me I woulda most definitely been there, right beside you. But on the other hand, if you need the God to fall back so you can do your own thing I can respect that, too. Let's let this shit burn for two more hours. Cool the flames and beat them bones to dust. Once all remnants are in the Hudson, we'll be good to go."

Kammron looked out at the garbage can again. "A'ight, that sound like a plan. I'ma do right by, Shana though, bruh. I ain't got no other choice. I'ma make sure she and this baby have everything they need as long as I'm alive. I don' fucked up so bad."

Bonkers stepped next to him and wrapped his arm around his shoulder. "It's gon' be all good, God. Just like everything else in life, this shall pass."

Shelly's skin, and muscles crackled and popped over and over. The loud sound of it came from inside of the garbage can and resonated to their ears. Kammron felt like breaking down to his knees from the stunt he'd pulled in taking her life. Bonkers also had a heavy heart. He didn't know what to say or do, so instead of coming down hard on Kammron about what was already done, he decided to take a different approach. One of support. That didn't mean he thought what Kammron did was right, but he was his brother in his heart. He knew he would ride with him through it all.

****

Later that night, Kammron pushed open the door to his father's room and found him sitting in a rocking chair staring out of the window. The sounds of Betty Davis crooned out of his old radio. He had a broad smile spread across his face. His gray afro missed a major patch in the middle. The room was small and decorated with only a lamp and a dresser. The bed was a twin. To the left was a bathroom with the door wide open. There was the aroma of piss coming from it.

Kammron closed the door behind him and stepped beside the rocking chair. "What's good, old man?"

Kendell looked over at his son. He stared at him for a long time with a smile on his face. Then it turned into a frown. He blinked his eyes a few times and mugged Kammron. "Li'l nigga what the fuck you doing here? I ain't got no muthafuckin' money, so don't ask."

Kammron felt offended. "Nigga, I don't need yo muthafuckin money. I'm out here eating like a nigga wit' a tapeworm, fuck you talking 'bout."

Kendell grunted. "Then what you want? The only time you come out here is when you need something." He turned up the Betty Davis record and tapped his hand on his thigh.

Kammron felt himself becoming heated. "Fuck you talking about? I ain't never asked you for shit. You been a dead beat ever since I came into this world. You ain't never did shit for me or my mother."

Kendell grunted again. "I ain't even sho you is my son boy, the way yo momma got around. Sometimes I think you is, sometimes I don't. Bottom line I ain't finna do shit for you, so you can keep it moving. You and yo mammy."

Kammron pulled a Glock from the small of his back. He screwed a silencer into the barrel. "Yo', all these years you been talking that bullshit, Kendell. Jaw jacking about my

moms, a get yo ass smoked quick, Pa, word to the heavens."
He cocked the pistol and held it at his side.

Kendell laughed. "Nigga, I'm paralyzed from the waist down. Been shot fifteen times and I'm still alive. I sit in this house all day and night, looking out of this window wondering what coulda been. What, you think cause you pull out a gun a muthafucka gon' be scared a something. Nigga this Harlem, right here fa real. You ain't said shit, aim that Bitch and fire Kammron. Put me out of my misery. I keep failing when I try to do it on my own." He reached for a cup of water that was set next to the lamp.

The lamplight illuminated the slashes that were up and down his arm. Both of his wrists had been slashed, along with his neck. Kendell had tried to kill himself more than twenty times. Each time he was brought back to life and made to sit in the crazy house.

Kammron shook his head. "Pops, I'm starting to feel that shit you got real bad. My depression is fucked up. I'm hot and cold, and I just want to kill all the time. I ain't got no feelings man, and all I think about is suicidal all day long. I'm drowning, and I need you to tell me how to deal with this shit."

Kendell rocked for a full minute. A smile slowly came across his face. "I ain't colored in my book all day. Need my graham crackers and juice. Then these people had the nerve to end slavery. Boy, at least we can flee to the north now, but I'm staying right here in the south, keeping it real. The Lord is my witness." He looked at Kammron. "Who the hell do you think you are?" he snapped.

Kammron ran his hand over his face. He knew he had to weather the storm. Most times his father's episodes of dementia, and illusions of grandeur only lasted for five minutes at a time. He'd started to become seriously mentally ill at the age of twenty-five. Kammron watched him rant on and on with

143

spit flying from his mouth for five minutes straight. Then he shook his head as hard as he could and faced Kammron.

"Yo', nigga is you back, now?" Kammron asked becoming frustrated. He tucked his gun into the small of his back.

Kendell sighed. "You just gotta let that shit take its course, Kamm. Of, course, you're my son you're going to struggle from time to time, but you'll get over it. If you don't, well you'll wind up here." He waved his arm around the room and started to laugh.

Kammron felt like pulling his gun back out and emptying the clip in Kendall's face. He hated the man for laughing at such a serious situation. Hated him for passing only dirty genes to himself.

Kendall scratched his nappy afro. "Don't you see that shit get the better of you. It's gon' make you wanna kill. It's gon' make you wanna cry. It's gon break you to your knees, but before it gets too bad, all you can do is end it. Shoot yourself, right here, Kid." He pointed to his temple. "End that shit li'l, nigga. That gene you got in you makes you dangerous, and pussy at the same time. Don't nobody wanna see them tears. Fuck ya feelings, get the fuck out of my room." He closed his eyes and smiled. "Sho can't wait to see how good, Michael Jordan gon' be. I hope he come to the Knicks. Ooo-we nineteen eighty-four gon be the year." He mused, digging in his nose.

Kammron turned his back to the man, feeling lower than he had ever mentally felt. He opened the door and left the room with his father ranting and raving behind him.

Chapter 17
Cleveland, Ohio

"Yo, tell me how this nigga, hook all this shit up from back in, New York?" Kammron asked, slipping into the blue Warner Cable jumpsuit.

Bonkers zipped up the one-piece jumpsuit that was identical to the one Kammron was wearing. The name tag stitched into the material over his right pocket read: *Sam.* "Yo', I don't know, but kid been pulling man strings for the last two months. We can't really complain cause, he got us eating like like pigs. Yo', I ain't know that Coke shit was still where it's at. I got so much money in the safe now it's hard for me to close that bitch. Pretty soon I'ma have to figure out what I'ma do wit' some of it."

Kammron tucked his guns inside of his jumpsuit. "Yo', I just like looking at my shits. I got two safes, one for the scratch, and the other for twenty-five bricks of Yay that Kid hit me wit' so far. A mafucka ain't been able to touch the white cuz Kid always got us out of town pulling shit like this. How the fuck we Kingpins, when all we do is whack shit?" He popped two Percocets and chased them down with bottled water. Then sat back in the passenger's seat of the mover's van and surveyed the neighborhood they were parked inside of.

It was a rainy day, two in the afternoon. The sun seemed to be hiding behind the thick dark clouds causing it to look as though it was night time instead of the afternoon.

Bonkers loaded up his weapons and sat behind the steering wheel of the van. "Yo', don't get me wrong, you most definitely got a point. Jimmy always hollering that Kingpin shit when it comes to all three of us, but the only nigga flipping that raw is him. He got us pushing wigs back on a weekly basis. I still can't understand how he got beef all the way in,

Ohio. But I'ma trust the process because we are eating." He started the van and pulled off.

Kammron felt the Percocets kicking in, he got that tingling feeling, and a smile came across his face. "Yo', I know it's only been a few months since the shit that happened with, Shelly, but Kid I think I'm starting to get a hold of myself. Me and Shana doing real. I just been trying to make her feel as good as possible. I ain't missed a doctor's appointment. Them weird cravings and shit that she starting to have be having the God all over New York copping word food items, but I be on it. I mean, I know I'm still bogus and all. Ain't nothing gon' change that, but I'm trying my best to make amends. This shit ain't easy though."

Bonkers continued to follow the GPS system on his phone. "They still wilding over Shelly's whereabouts?"

The Percocets really kicked in for Kammron now, he felt slow—numb. His body was vibrating in a good way. He wiped his nose. "Yeah, Dunn, especially Stacie. Ever since shorty been missing, she ain't been right. I can see that shit all in her face. Yo', would you believe that sometimes I be wanting to sit her down and confess. That grief written on her face be killing me, Kid. Word up, she looks like she losing weight and everything.

"Shana taking that shit in stride. She's convinced that Shelly coming back and that she just bounced on her own accord because that is what she used to tell her, she was going to do all the time. I think she's more focused on the love and affection I show her. That's the only thing that matters. Yo', enough about me, though. What's good with my, niece man? And how are you and Yasmin getting along?"

Bonkers shrugged his shoulders. "We good, Kid, with respects to me and, Yazzy. Yo', my word, that's the love of my life. I'd do anything for that, baby girl. It feels like I fall in love with her more and more every single day. It's one of the best feelings in the world."

"Yo', she mad beautiful too, Dunn. I still can't figure out how she turned out so pretty with ya ugly ass wrapped up in her DNA like that?" Kammron snickered, his eyelids were so heavy, he had to force them open.

"Ha-ha-ha, nigga. Yo', I'm the reason, she as pretty as she is. Let's get that straight, right now." He made a left and followed the arrow of the GPS system.

"I was just fucking wit' you, Kid, it's all love. What's up wit' you and Yasmin. You still hollering this faithful shit or what?"

Bonkers was quiet for a minute. "I ain't never said I was on no faithful shit. I ain't trying to put no labels on nothing we're doing. I'm simply taking it day by day, and so far, so good. Yasmin is worthy of the best man I can be to her. Her and Yazzy have been through a lot without me. So, while they have me, I just want to assure that things are smooth as possible for them. I care about her, Kammron. Yasmin, I mean, like I really care about that girl, B."

Kammron nodded his head. "Yo', that's your baby mother, Dunn. You're supposed to care about her, that's a good thing. But that don't mean you stop getting pussy, though. Hers only gon' feel some type of way for so long. In a matter of time you gon' be fiending for a different snatch, and then what?"

Bonkers kept rolling, he turned the windshield wipers on highly. The rain was coming down as if they had entered into some kind of tropical storm. "Yo,' I still get those urges for other women. I think every man do, it's just the way we're designed. And I ain't saying that one day I ain't gon' act on those urges, but, right now it ain't about the pussy. It's about making sure my daughter sees both of her parents together in a loving, positive, and strong relationship. It's about stability and being with a woman you can trust. These streets are so cutthroat now that you don't know who you can and can't trust."

Kammron scoffed. "Yo', and you really think you can trust her?"

Bonkers took a second and nodded his head. "For the most part. I mean she ain't gave me no reason not to. I'm pretty certain our goals are lined up. We want what's best for, Yazzy. She is what's most important. Sooner or later you'll establish that bond with, Shana. It's imperative that you do."

"You got me fucked up. I don't even trust my own mama, never the less a bitch outside of her." Kammron sat all the way up in his seat. "Yo', if it's one thing Harlem taught us, is that you can never trust a Bitch or one of these cutthroat ass niggas. But a Bitch a do you in quicker than a nigga will. I got mad respect for, Shana and Stacie as well, but trusting them ain't part of the equation. Never that!"

Kammron's words had Bonkers second-guessing his thoughts. He had to admit he could remember hearing about more stories about females setting niggas up to be robbed and whacked than he did any others. Harlem had taught them that putting all of your trust into a female would do you in, in the long run. He imagined Yasmin's face in his mind. Thought about how things had been between them ever since they'd gotten back in tune with each other. In his opinion, they were in a good space and building ground.

They were focused on giving Yazzy the strongest two parent household they could build for her. When it came to themselves, they were looking to remain cordial. They didn't want to put any labels on things, but it was as if they had an unspoken understanding that they were together, and each party knew what was expected of the other. They felt solid. He didn't know how much he trusted her, but he was sure he did. He just couldn't see her betraying him for any reason. That wasn't even her track record.

"Yo', fuck yo' WiFi shut off or some shit? You been sitting at this stop sign for two minutes." Kammron mugged him and looked both ways.

"N'all, Son, it's good. I just had some shit on my mind, that's all." Bonkers pulled past the stop sign still lost deep within his thoughts.

He thought it was in his best interest to keep his thoughts, and comments to himself. The more Kammron talked the more he started to second guess his decisions. He felt he needed to go with his gut. To continue to give Yasmin, and their relationship a chance. He owed that to Yazzy if no one else.

"Yo', Bonkers, I ain't mean to rain on ya parade a nothin'. If you and shorty rocking all good and what not, then you gotta see that shit through. I just ain't there yet wit', Shana, that's all." He looked out of his passenger's window.

Bonkers glanced over to him and threw the van in park. "Yo', Kid, what made you say that shit?"

Kammron laughed. "Nigga I been knowing since I uttered my first words. I can tell when something ain't right wit' ya ass. Plus, when it comes to Yasmin, I see how good she make you feel. Ya crazy about ya lil Princess and all of that. The God a be foul as hell if I took that away from you with my ill feelings toward bitches in general. That ain't cool, so I apologize."

Bonkers waved him off. "Now you going too far, it's good B. We were raised in the trenches of Uptown. It's what we were taught. I can't hold that shit against you. You feel how you feel."

Kammron tapped him on the shoulder. "Yo', here comes one of the marks, right now, be smooth." Kammron slid his leather gloves on his hands and popped the collar to his uniform. He could feel the weight of the pistols poking against his rib cage.

Bonkers eyed the heavy-set, red-faced man as he made his way down the driveway smoking a cigar. The rain beaded down all around him. Bonkers grew giddy, he was ready to pull the move and get back to New York. He was missing Yazzy and knew she was asking about him and where he was.

The mark ran over and knocked on the window. He waited until Bonkers rolled it down just enough. "Hey, are you the guys?" He asked looking into Bonkers' face.

Kammron came and slid the back door to the side. "Man get yo' punk ass in so you can tell us what's going on."

The man jumped into the back of the van and slammed the door behind him. "Look, fellas, Charlie, and Jerry are inside. They're getting ready to host a high stakes poker game where a few heavy hitters are set to show up. When these heavy hitters do come, they are going to have much of security. It would be wise for us to strike now. I'll escort you inside as the cable men because, right now, I've screwed with the reception so that it looks scrambled. You two will come in and get right to work. They won't suspect a thing."

Bonkers eyed him closely. He didn't like the fact that the heavyset man had a habit of spitting when he talked. "Yo, when you and Jimmy linking up, anyway?" he wanted to know.

The man scoffed. "'That isn't any of your concern. You were sent here to handle a job. Be professional and do exactly that. Now let's go, time is money, and I'm giving Jimmy a whole lot for this move." He opened the door and stepped back out into the rain.

Kammron mugged Bonkers. "Yo', I'll lace that punk, Kid. Who the fuck that fat nigga think he talking to?" Kammron felt his heart beating fast.

Bonkers' was beating just as fast and hard. He sucked his teeth and nodded his head. "Yo', leave his bitch ass to me. Jimmy already said this fool gotta go too. So, let's handle this bidness." He rolled back up the window, and they stepped out of the van.

****

The fat man entered into the living room with two glasses of lemonade. He looked over his shoulder, then back at both Kammron and Bonkers, who were kneeled behind the big screen television acting as if they were really fixing it.

"Okay, there are three men and one woman sitting at the table. All are snorting coke. The three men have to be taken care of. The woman is my wife. She walks away from that table intact. Do you understand me? You touch one red hair on her head and Jimmy will be missing two of his men. That's a promise—now go." He pointed toward the next room of the house where a table had been set up for the bosses to play Poker.

Bonkers trigger finger was itching horribly. He didn't like the fat man. He was ready to put two in his melon. "A'ight, we got you, Kid, let's go, bruh."

Kammron stood up with a mug on his face. He glared at the fat man. "Yeah, let's roll." He pulled both .45s out of his uniform and rushed into the living room. As soon as he stepped inside, it was like all eyes were on him. The fat man's wife's eyes got big. She opened her mouth to scream, while one of the bosses reached for his 9mm. Kammron started to finger fuck his pistols back to back. His first bullets landed into the man's wife's and knocked her brains out. She was dead before she fell out of her chair. His fourth, fifth, and sixth bullets shredded apart the first Boss's face as the man looked to aim his gun at him.

Bonkers rushed inside of the room picking up where Kammron left off. His bullets came fast and plentiful. He fucked his triggers as if they were new pussy. The entire room filled with gun smoke. Shells dropped to the carpet along with the bodies of the bosses.

"Oh my, God! Oh my, God! You idiot, you shot my wife! You shot my fuckin' wife!" The fat man hollered, running up on Kammron.

Bonkers stepped in his path, held his arm straight out, placed the barrel to the man's forehead and pulled the trigger three times. His noodles spilled against the wall. As he was falling backward Bonkers hit him four more times. By the time he landed on the carpet, he was lifeless. Bonkers pulled a black Hefty garbage bag out of his underwear and dumped all the work from a table inside it. Then he rushed to the deep freezer and threw all the frozen food that was on top of the coke out of it, before discovering the bricks at the bottom of it just like Jimmy said there would be. Kammron rushed to his side, and both men emptied the freezer, before breaking out of the house, and out of Cleveland.

Chapter 18

A week later, Kammron stepped into his apartment at two in the morning. After a joyous night at the strip club, to find Shana sitting on his couch with her head down. The only light in the house was a lamp that was set right on the side of the couch. He closed the door and adjusted his vision. The three Percocets and Patron had him fucked up. He swallowed his spit and ran his hand over his face.

Shana raised her head. "Hey, Kamm, I bet you surprised to see me here, huh?"

Kammron staggered into the house and rested his shoulder on the wall. "Yo', how the fuck you get in my crib shorty?"

Shana held up a key. "Since you ain't give me one, I had one made at the bodega on the corner down there. It shouldn't be a big deal."

Kammron waved her off. "Yo', it ain't but you shoulda still asked me." He scratched his inner forearm. "So, what's up?"

Shana sighed and ran her fingers through her hair. "Killa, I need to know what's good wit' us, B? Yo', you so hot and cold that I don't be knowing what to think. Are we going to be together for this baby, or what?"

Kammron staggered into the kitchen and opened the re-frigerator. "I ain't ate shit all day, I'm hungrier than a hostage." He pulled out a box of KFC, opened the microwave, tossed it inside and put it on two minutes.

Shana exhaled loudly, stood up, walked into the kitchen, turned on the sink, and filled her a glass with water. She took a sip and eyed him over the rim.

Kammron peeped her. "Fuck yo' problem? I just said I was hungry." He popped the microwave back open even though it had thirty seconds before it finished, took out the box, and drenched the chicken in hot sauce. Then he picked up a thigh and shred it with his teeth like a savage.

"Kammron, stop playing wit' me and answer my question. I need to know what you gon' do because I'm tired of worrying myself crazy. If you ain't gon' be wit' me, I'm gon' find somebody that will. It's as simple as that." She turned her back to him and walked out of the kitchen.

Kammron continued to smack loudly. He sucked the hot sauce off his fingers and swallowed a bite of chicken. Then he jerked his head back and dropped the chicken into the box. He wiped his hand on the dish rag and walked into the living room. "Yo', what the fuck you want from me, shorty? Ain't I handling all of ya cravings, buying you maternity clothes and all of that shit?"

Shana nodded. "Yeah, you doing all of that."

"Bitch, don't every time I see you, I make sure your pockets are fat? Don't I pay all of your mother's bills? Got both of y'all driving trucks and shit, fresh off the lot? Ain't a mafucka doing all of that?"

Shana hopped up. "Nigga, yeah, you doing all that financial shit. And what? That's your job as a man. Don't try and throw that shit in my face." She rolled her eyes.

Kammron stepped into her face. "Bitch, who the fuck you talking too like that? You better watch yo muthafuckin' tone before I beat yo' li'l ass."

Shana lowered her head. "Kammron, I know you crazy and all that shit, but on my mother, I ain't scared of you."

Kammron clenched his jaw off and on. He felt himself fuming. "Yo', you ain't gotta be scared of me, but you gon most definitely respect me."

She sucked her teeth. "Man, boy bye." She turned her back to him. "Niggas, be thinking just because they drop a few chips it makes them entitled to a certain level of respect, and

154

prestige. Ownership of a woman and shit. I'm pregnant, I'm about to have your child. Nigga, you supposed to be doing everything you're doing if you have the means to do so. I mean I appreciate it and all that shit, but I'm not impressed. I need you more than financially. I need you physically, emotionally, and spiritually. A woman needs stability and security. She needs to know she will be taken care of and protected for the long haul. So, you think you can throw money at me, and that's going to appease my needs. I demand you treat me like a Queen, once again, I'm having your kid."

Kammron mugged her for a long time. She was blowing his high. Shelly's face came to his mind. He remembered the promise he'd made her to do right by Shana. He had to stick to that. It was the least he could do after taking her life. "Yo', shorty, so what do you want from me? What would make you most happy, right now?"

Shana placed her right hand on her stomach. "I just ain't trying to be a statistic, Killa. I want us to raise our child together. I need you to treat me like Queen instead of a bitch. You walk around all day calling yourself a God. Well as a woman under you do you know that I am supposed to be your, church? You're supposed to be sacrificial for me. Instead, you treat me like an average every day, run of the mill Harlem guttersnipe. That has to stop."

Kammron went and flopped on the couch. He laid all the way back and stared at the ceiling. "Yo', this shit way harder than I thought it was gon' be. The kid turned nineteen in a few weeks, and it's like life already whooping my ass. I got a lot of growing up to do, shorty. I ain't got all the answers."

Shana stepped up to the couch and looked down on him. "I don't expect you, too. But there is one thing I need to ask you. One thing I know you have the answer to."

Kammron closed his eyes and yawned. "Yeah, shorty, I got love for you. I care about you and all of that. You ain't even gotta ask that question." He made himself a bit more comfortable. "That what you wanted to ask me?"

Shana swallowed her spit. "Kammron, what happened to my sister?" She couldn't believe the words had come out of her mouth, but she needed and craved answers.

Kammron slowly sat up. "What you say?"

Shana cleared her throat, she felt like she was getting ready to cry again. She really missed Shelly, and now it was clear she was no longer off doing her own thing. In Shana's mind, she was missing, and she was sure Kammron had something to do with it. She didn't know his level of involvement, but something was fishy.

"I'm asking you to keep shit real with me, Kamm. Tell me what happened to, my sister?"

Kamm jumped up, he wished he wasn't so fuckin' high. Had he not been, he woulda been able to mentally manipulate her with ease. Due to the fact that the Percocets were fuckin' with his brain, he couldn't think straight. "Shorty, why would you even ask me some shit like that? You gotta know, I don't know." He mugged her, as the murder of Shelly played over and over in his mind.

"I ain't buying that shit, Killa. Nigga, I know how you get down in these Uptown streets. Yo', name ring alarms all around here. If you ain't have nothing to do with Shelly's disappearance you would have torn this city up already. That's one thing I do know. So, far you been laid back with everything. I know you cared about my sister. I can't see an animal like you handling shit so lightly. So, what's really good?"

"Yo', I don't know, stop asking me about that shit. I miss her just as much as you do. That was my baby." He felt his eyes tearing up. He tried to shake it off, wishing he hadn't mixed his Purks with Mollies. The Molly had that emotional shit coming out of him.

"Kammron, you can tell me, daddy. I just need emotional closure. If I knew what happened to her, then I could move on with my life. I mean I've already made my peace that she's dead. But how? Did she do something to you? Did she find out about us, and you had to get rid of her?"

Kammron felt the first tears drip down his face. They dropped off his chin. "Yo', I loved Shelly man. Quit asking me all these stupid ass questions, Shana. That was my baby."

'Was?' Shana thought. *Damn, so my sister is dead.*

She felt sick to her stomach, she wanted to scream. She had to get everything out of him. It would be the only way she could prevent herself from going crazy. "Talk to me, Kammron. I mean I have your baby inside of me. It's just you and I for the long haul. We have to become one. Whatever types of secrets you're harboring you can release them into me. I swear I won't tell nobody else, Daddy. Look at me!"

The Mollies were fully taking over now. Kammron shoulda never taken the pills on an empty stomach. Tears ran down his cheeks. His bipolar started to rise to the surface, along with his depression. "Yo', Shelly gone, Shana, leave her where she is. Ain't no sense in us talking about her no more."

Shana grabbed a hold of his shirt and balled it into her fists. "Tell me what happened, Kammron? Please, I know you know what happened to my sister. It's killing me, please tell me—I am begging you. *What happened?*" She smacked him as hard as she could and pushed him.

Kammron went flying backward, he fell over the table and hit his head. The blow knocked a good part of his common sense from him immediately. That worked against him in conjunction with his mental illness, and the heavy drug usage.

Before he could control his brain, he was laughing out loud. "You, stupid bitch." He jumped up.

Shana backed toward the front door. Her shirt rose above her pregnant belly. "I'm sorry, Kammron, I didn't mean to put my hands on you. I'm just—"

Kammron lowered his eyes. "Shit happens, in this game, in this world. In relationships, it just fucking happens. His face was wet with tears. I promised her before she died that I was gon' do right by you." He squeezed his eyelids tighter. "I promised her things would be different. But she was gon' leave me anyway man. She didn't care about me no more. All-cause of what you and I did. Then we got to arguing and fighting and shit. By the time she tried to console me I was too far gon'. I knew she would never come back."

Shana shook her head. "Kammron, you didn't, please tell me you didn't." She backed toward the couch and sank down it."

Kammron held out his arms like a cross. "This is me, Shana. This the nigga you getting ready to have a baby by. Bitch, I'm fucked up in the head, I'm nuts!" More tears came out of his eyes.

"What did you do, Kammron, huh? What did you do to, Shelly?" she cried.

"I choked the bitch out, both hands." He demonstrated and shook his hands back and forth. "She was fighting me and begging me to stop. Smacking at my hands and shit. But I kept on choking harder and harder until she was lifeless. Because that's what happens when you try and leave me in this darkness. I didn't wanna be left alone." He rushed to the couch and piled the .357 Magnum from under it, spun the cylinder, and aimed it at Shana. Then he cocked the hammer and smiled. His right eye twitched, Shana was a blur in his vision. A voice in his head told him to pull the trigger—to kill her.

Coke Kings

Shana stood up and held her hands in front of her. "Whoa-whoa-whoa, Kamm. There is no need to do this. I just wanted to know what happened. You've told me, now I know. We can move on!"

Kammron shook his. "N'all, bitch, it's too late for that. You know too much. I can't just let you just walk out of here with that knowledge. How smart would that be?"

Shana blinked tears. "Kammron, this isn't you, right now. You don't want to do this, baby. There is something going on in your mind, and I understand it's not your fault. I swear I won't hold this against you."

Kammron aimed and pulled the trigger. *Click!* "Tell me something, Shana? What made you fuck your sister's man, huh? What made you go behind that bitch back and fuck me?" He extended his arm and aimed at her again.

Shana felt like she was ready to piss herself, sweat slid down the side of her forehead. "I don't know, Kammron. I just liked you a whole lot. I didn't care that she was my sister. All I could think about was the sexual side of things "

Kammron blinked ten times fast, his vision was hazy. "Yousa sheisty, bitch." He pulled the trigger. *Click!*

Shana jumped in the air and really did piss down her thigh. "Kammron, Please, don't do this shit! You're driving me crazy. I already told you I would never tell. You need to trust me."

Kammron spun the cylinder again. "Trust no man, trust no bitch, trust no hoe, trust no nigga. Bitches ain't shit but hoes and tricks. So, kill 'em. Bitch, I'm Killa Kamm, it's Harlem." He squeezed his eyelids together, and the gun began to shake in his hand. "It ain't just my fault, Shana, it's yours too. We both brought this shit on ourselves. So, after I kill you, I'ma kill myself. That's what Shelly woulda wanted." He placed his finger on the trigger again.

Shelly jumped up and rushed him as fast as she could and tackled him into the table. He fell over it and hit his head on the arm of the couch, hard. It caused his neck to pop in an awkward position. The gun slid across the floor. Kammron groaned as a slight tingle rushed up and down his spine. Now he was dizzier than ever as he struggled to make it to his feet. He stood in front of the door trying to gather himself.

Shana looked for an exit route of escape. Kammron was standing in front of the door. To her, he seemed disoriented. She looked down at the floor, spotted the gun and looked back up at him. Kammron had both of his hands on his head trying to stop from throwing up.

"Kammron, please just let me go. I won't say anything. You're absolutely right. Her death was both of our faults. I won't put this solely on you, you, have to trust me. We're going to have a child to raise. Shana didn't know what she was going to do yet, but one thing was for sure, she knew she needed to get the hell out of Kammron's apartment.

There were loud bells going off inside of Kammron's head. He could barely hear what she was saying, and his vision was even worse. He fell to his knees and held his stomach. He waved her off and proceeded to throw up.

Shana rushed around him, kicked the gun away, and opened the door, rushing out of it happy to be alive. She didn't know what her next move would be, but for now, it was to breathe a sigh of relief.

Chapter 19

Yasmin stepped into the bedroom hugging the sheer, purple, Victoria Secrets robe around her body. She could hear the *Ella Mai's* album crooning out of the speakers, as she stood in front of Bonkers. He sat on the edge of the bed shirtless. The blue light from the lamp illuminated his abs and muscular chest. To her, he looked like an African God. She could feel the anticipation and excitement build between her thighs. She took two steps back and opened the robe.

Then dropped it to the floor. "You like what you see, baby?"

Bonkers looked her over with a slight smile on his face. He saw the way the tight purple panties clung to her V, cuffing the mound so righteous that he could make out both of her sex lips. A hint of her skin was exposed on each side. Her chocolate thighs glistened. They were freshly rubbed down with scented lotion, a coat of baby oil applied on top of them. Her sexy stomach was decorated with a few traces of stretch marks that looked so sexy.

Sexy because they had come from the making of his daughter. "Yo, my word Goddess, I ain't never seen nobody sexier in my life. Give me one more circle, so I can really see what you're working with."

She rolled her eyes. "As if you didn't know." She slowly turned in a circle for him.

Bonkers waited until she stopped directly in front of him and pulled her between his legs by grabbing a hold of her backside. He kissed her stomach from his seated position, licked circles around her belly button, and sucked the skin there. "I love his stomach, boo."

She smiled. "You better, it's all yours."

He unhooked her bra from the front and allowed it to fall off her shoulders. Then he cupped her breasts and squeezed them. His thumbs went back and forth across her nipples until they were nice and hard. Then he started sucking them one at a time while rubbing her box.

Yasmin spaced her thighs open, tilted her head back and moaned. "Unnhhh, Bonkers, you trying to heat me up?"

His fingers pulled the material to the side. Her bare lips exposed themselves. His middle digit played in between her crease. He was met by wetness, it seeped out of her, and on to his fingers. He sucked his digits into his mouth, picked her up by the waist and sat her on the bed.

He scooted her back to the middle of it and opened her thighs wide. "Let me get these panties off of you."

Yasmin raised her ass from the bed while he slipped her panties off, leaving her naked and exposed. She opened her thighs wider in preparation. "Come get you some, Bonkers."

Bonkers stripped at the foot of the bed. His dick slapped against his thigh as he crawled back on the mattress. His nose wound up in her box, sniffing her essence. The scent caused him to shake like crazy. He loved the smell of her pussy, he couldn't help how it affected him. Yasmin held her pussy lips open while his tongue traced up and down her slit. He sucked one lip into his mouth at a time. Then diddled her clitoris, before sucking it into his mouth. He was licking and sucking her like a savage for ten minutes straight.

Yasmin humped into his mouth and moaned loudly. She squeezed her titties together and pulled on the hard nipples pulling them from her mounds. When his fingers entered her box, she could no longer take it. She cried out, arched her back, and came hard running her tongue all over her lips.

Bonkers slurped her pussy juices as they seeped out of her. The saltiness drove him mad he was addicted to the taste. He

Coke Kings

sucked her juices off her thighs, and from the crack of her ass,
then licked all the way back up to her clit, treating it like an
oyster.

Yasmin bucked hard and sucked on her finger. "Baby,
please, please put it in me now! I'm thirsty for it, I need you in
me, right now." She trailed her hand between her thighs and
pinched her clit. This sent a jolt through her.

Bonkers climbed up her body stroking his dick. He eyed
her puffy pussy lips and felt like he wanted to spew his seed.
Her thighs were splayed widely. He kissed her shoulder, and
bite into it and licked his tongue along her collarbone before
his hand slipped between her legs.

"Baby, you already know what I need. I need a lil bit of
that Harlem Shake." He laid on his back and stroked his piece
up and down.

Yasmin crawled to her knees and took him in her hand,
then stroked him up and down. She kissed his head and sucked
it into her mouth like a chicken bone. Her tongue licked up
and down the slit at the top of it. She popped him out loudly
and licked all over it. "You like that, baby?"

Bonkers' toes were curled up. "Hell, yeah, I do. Handle
that bidness, boo."

That was all that needed to be said. Yasmin swallowed
half of him and brought her mouth to the top of his head, then
took him to the base again before her head was in his lap. She
sucked, slurped, added extra spit, and licked it up, going to
work on him.

Bonkers smacked that ass and ran his finger up and down
her slit. He played with her sex lips, separated them, and eased
a middle finger into her box. Her tunnel was nice, tight, and
scorching. He pulled it out and sucked it into his mouth while
she went into a frenzy on his tool.

T.J. Edwards

Yasmin reached under her stomach and tweaked her clit. She rubbed circles around her pearl, and her thighs began to shake. The feel of his dick in her mouth, him playing with her sex, and the pinching of her clit became too much. She jerked, and came hard, sucked him with all of her might, pumping her fist up and down his length.

Bonkers humped up from the bed He smelled the scent of her pussy in the air, felt her titties on his thighs. The erect nipples piercing him. She slurped and smacked, and the audio pushed him over the edge. He growled and came hard, while she continued to suck him.

Yasmin felt the warm jets hitting the back of her throat. They caught her off guard, she swallowed and continued to suck him faster and faster, loving the taste of his cream.

Bonkers pulled out and got between her thighs. He rubbed his dick up and down her slit, coating it with her juices. "Yo', this my pussy, right here, baby. This shit belongs to me, right?" His big head played with her sex flaps, more essence oozed out of her, and created a shiny sheen at the crack of her ass.

"You damn right it is. I belong to you, Bonkers. Now fuck me, Daddy. Fuck me like you run this pussy." She scooted down and opened her thighs even wider. Her pussy lips were fully engorged. Her clitoris sat at the top of her hood like a bell.

Bonkers slowly eased into her valley. When his dick was about four inches in, he slammed the last five and a half home hard.

"Uhhh!" Yasmin yelped as a trimmer traveled through her.

Bonkers pushed her knees to her chest and started long stroking that pussy fast and hard. It was so wet that with every stroke there was a loud noise coming from between her legs that sounded like somebody walking on wet plastic with their shoes on.

Bonkers began to growl. "Mmm-mmm-mmm-mmm-arrgh. This-my-pussy, I'll-kill-a-nigga—Over-dis—pussy!" He growled fucking harder and harder.

Yasmin's head went from right to left on her neck. "Daddy, ooo-ooo-ooo-fuck me! Fuck me-yes-yes-yes—uunnhhhh! Baby-baby, beat this shit up-beat it up—aw-www—yes!"

Bonkers rolled his back hard, he tightened his grip. His dick plunged deeper and deeper. "I'll kill a nigga over you. I'll-kill-a-nigga-over-you." Every time he heard the words come out of his mouth, it made him fuck her harder and harder.

Her breathing was rugged, it was like the pussy got better and better with every stroke. He could barely contain himself.

"Baby, ooo—fuck!" He growled splashing her walls back to back.

Yasmin felt his cum hitting her walls. A strong tremor surfed through her clitoris. Before she could cum, he was flipping her onto her stomach and opening her ass. His tongue traveled in circles around her rosebud. Then his tongue snuck inside. She slid her fingers under her stomach and began playing with her juicy pussy. His tongue darted in and out of her back door. He smacked her hand away, pulled her up to her knees, and slid into her pussy from the back fucking her like a savage.

"Gimme, dis—shit!" he roared.

She laid her face on the bed while he took her. Her juicy booty crashed into his lap back to back. It jiggled and sucked his dick. She was leaking, her lips squeezed his pole, and tried to trap him inside of her over and over.

"Daddy-Daddy, ooo-you-hitting this shit! Ooo son, you hitting this shit—unnhhhh-unnhhhh, Daddeee!" she screamed cumming hard.

Bonkers got to fucking her so hard, sweat was dripping off of his chin. His teeth were clenched together. The headboard beat into the wall loudly. She whimpered underneath him and came again. The feel of her insides vibrating sent him off. He came with a burst of semen and fell on top of her jumping away.

Yasmin moved her booty backward to assist him. Sweat dripped off her chin, and ear lobes. She loved the way Bonkers beat her pussy up. She was as born and bred in Harlem and needed that Uptown shit. The harder he fucked her the more at home she felt. "Fuck this pussy, Daddy. Fuck it-fuck it-awww shit fuck me!"

Bonkers laid on his side and slid in and out of her. He gripped her right breast and pulled it back to his mouth. Then trapped the nipple, fast stroking her pussy for another fifteen minutes until both of them came.

****

Yasmin laid on the side of him rubbing his stomach muscles. The room smelled like hot sex, and perfume. Bonkers gripped her booty, kneaded the globes in his hand like dough, before trailing his finger up and down her crack. Yasmin continued to ooze out of her box.

"You wanna know what's crazy, Bonkers? And I hope this don't ruin the moment," she started, looking into his eyes.

Bonkers slipped a finger back into her pussy, he relished the feel of the heat that resonated from there. "Yo', what's that?"

"I already knew ever since we were kids that you and I were meant for each other. Like seriously, ever since I was a little girl there had never been another boy that has made me feel like you did. That same feeling is still evident, right here today. I love you, Bonkers, I mean fa real fa real! I hope we last for a long time whenever we do decide to take that next step." She smiled and ran her finger over his lips.

Bonkers smiled. "Yo', I love you too, Boo. Even though I ain't wit' putting labels on everything, yo' with all of my heart I'm riding for you, ma. The God is fully invested in you, and our daughter. I'm on my manly shit fa real, word to Janine."

Yasmin giggled. "I always find that so funny when you and Kammron be saying the names of y'alls mother's when y'all swear on something. I find that very amusing." She kissed his lips. "But I hear you baby, and I just wanted to let you know, I'm riding for you just as hard. I don't see nobody else but you, and there is no other man deserving of our family than you. I appreciate your every sacrifice. I got your back one hundred percent." She straddled his waist and sat up with her hands in his chest. She looked into his handsome face and smiled. "So, I'm saying, are you thinking about putting a ring on my finger, orrrr—" She held them out and wiggled them.

Bonkers laughed. "Yo', you know what? A man ain't never supposed to make a woman a mother before he makes her a wife. My grandmother always told me that. Being that I already dropped the ball on that whole theory it's best that I as a man right that wrong. So, what you thinking, like three carats?"

Yasmin squealed and hugged his neck as hard as she could. Tears spilled out of her eyes, and she couldn't help it.

"Oh, baby, you make me so happy. I don't even know what to say. I'm just so happy for our family." She hugged him tighter.

"Yo', it's what I'm supposed to do as a man. You ain't gotta worry about shit from here on out. That's my word."

She kissed his lips. "Word to Janine, right, baby?"

Bonkers busted out laughing. "Word to Janine."

Chapter 20

Early the next morning, Kammron began beating on the door to Bonkers' apartment. "Yo', open up, Kid. Open the damn door." He beat some more.

Bonkers grabbed the Tech-9 from under the bed and rushed to put his shorts on. Once they were on, he turned to Yasmin who was looking him over terrified. "Yo', stay ya ass in here. I don't give a fuck how long I'm in the other room you stay your ass, right in here. Do we understand each other?"

She nodded. "Baby, what if it's the police? Then what do we do?" she asked nervously.

"Anything they worried about you tell them muthafuckas you don't know shit, and they need to holler at me. You don't try and be a fuckin' hero. You got that?"

"I got that, baby. Can you kiss me before you go in there though?" She came to her knees and reached out for him.

Kammron started to beat so hard on the door that some of Bonkers' neighbors stuck their head out of their doors to see what all of the ruckus was about. After he mugged them, they slammed their doors back and locked them.

Bonkers finished tonguing Yasmin down. He kissed her lips and licked all over them. "A'ight Boo, chill in here. Matter fact get on the floor in case some shooting starts."

Yasmin dropped to the floor and followed his directives. She couldn't lie to herself and say she wasn't scared because she was terrified. "Be careful, baby."

Bonkers nodded and stepped into the hallway, closing the door behind him. He came to the side of his front door with the Tech in his hand. "Yo', who the fuck is it beating on my door like you crazy?"

Kammron kicked the door. "Nigga, it's me, open this mafucka," he snapped.

169

.J. Edwards

Bonkers took the locks off of the door. "Fuck you beating on the door like you the Feds for?"

Kammron rushed in with his head lowered. "Damn, nigga, you got me waiting out there all day and shit." He walked into the living room and paced back and forth.

Bonkers could fell something was wrong with him right away. He locked the door back. "Yo', what the fuck happened, Kid? I can see that shit written all over your face."

"That bitch know, B." Kammron continued to pace. His right hand rested on the back of his neck.

"What bitch, and what are you talking about that she knows?"

"Shana, she knows, I iced Shelly man. We just had this big thing, and now she just knows man. I fucked up, I'm losing my mind. I don't know what to do. I gotta kill her, right?" He stopped and looked over to Bonkers for confirmation.

Bonkers frowned and balled his fists. "Yo', how the fuck she find out? Don't tell me you opened that big ass mouth of yours?"

Kammron nodded. "That fuckin' Mollie and Percocets don't mix, Bonkers. But I been putting that tar up my nose, and I feel so much better. But now this bitch is in the wind. She fucked me up, too. Got my neck all fucked up and what-not. Yo', I'm vexed, I gotta kill her right?" he asked this again.

Bonkers shook his head. He didn't know what to do or say. "Bruh, damn, so you just started running ya big ass mouth cause you was hopped up on a few pills? Fuck type of shit is that? And where she at now?"

"We got into this big fight, then she ran out of the door. She kept saying she wasn't gon' say shit about her sister mur-der, but I don't know. That gotta be a tough pill to swallow."

Bonkers massaged his temples and took a deep breath. "We burned shorty to the bone, then beat them bitches to dust.

They don't stand a chance at finding her. But you had to open up your fucking mouth. Yo', you constantly screwing us over, Kid. What the fuck?" Bonkers slumped on the couch, lost and pissed off.

Yasmin covered her mouth at hearing how both of them had handled Shelly. The story sent chills down her spine. She also couldn't believe Bonkers had been a part of it. She wondered if he had any part in the actual killing of her. Her and Shelly had been good friends ever since she was nine years old. Her ending sounded tragic. It made Yasmin question everything, including her and Yazzy's safety for the long haul.

"Yo', you already know I didn't mean to, Kid. When have you ever known me to spill the beans about anything?"

"Right the fuck now, nigga, damn!" Bonkers hopped up. "Yo', we gotta find her like asap. Ain't no telling who she talking, too, or what she finna do with that information. She could be sitting in front of twelve right now as we speak."

Kammron ran his hand over his face. "Damn, man, fuck." He placed his back on the wall. "I fucked up, Bonkers. I fucked all the way up. I shoulda killed her—I shoulda killed her as soon as I let that shit slip out of my mouth."

Yasmin waited patiently with her hand over her mouth to see what Bonkers' response was going to be to this. She prayed he would tell him that was a bad idea. That Shelly's family had suffered enough. That more murder was not the answer to their problem. Or he would remind him that Shana was pregnant with his child, and taking her life meant he would also be taking the life of their child. She prayed he spoke in the positive. That if Kammron had killed Shelly he would convince him to turn himself in. Oh, how she prayed for any of these desired responses. She stood up and opened the door just a tad so she could hear them better.

"Yo', that is your mess to clean up. I can't tell you what to do, but you already know they gon' lace your ass over her murder, Kid. On the other hand, Shana got your seed. You whack her, you bodying your shorty, too. Like I said I can't micromanage what you do, but whatever we finna do we gotta get a move on like, right now."

"I gotta kill that bitch, B. It's the only way, if Stacie finds out I killed her daughter not only would she never forgive me, but she'd have them put me up under the jail. I can't stomach that, both of them might have to go."

Yasmin was listening so hard she slipped fell in the hall-way. "Aw shit," she hollered.

Kammron upped two Glocks and rushed down the hall. He pointed both of them at Yasmin. "Yo', this Bitch was eaves-dropping the whole time. Hell, n'all, Kid that's one too many witnesses."

Yasmin held her hands in the air. "Baby, come get yo crazy ass friend!"

Bonkers sprint down the hallway. "Kammron, what the fuck is you doing, Kid? Take them guns off her." He upped the Tech and aimed it down the hall at Kammron's back. "Kammron, don't!"

Kammron shook his head and cocked the hammers. "N'all, fuck that, this bitch getting between us anyway. If we smoking Shana, then she gotta go, too. We gotta get this money. Fuck these hoes. It's always been us, Dunn, until this bitch came along." His finger slipped around the trigger.

Boom!

To Be Continued...
Coke Kings 2
Coming Soon

Submission Guideline

Submit the first three chapters of your completed manuscript to ldpsubmissions@gmail.com, subject line: Your book's title. The manuscript must be in a .doc file and sent as an attachment. Document should be in Times New Roman, double spaced and in size 12 font. Also, provide your synopsis and full contact information. If sending multiple submissions, they must each be in a separate email.

Have a story but no way to send it electronically? You can still submit to LDP/Ca$h Presents. Send in the first three chapters, written or typed, of your completed manuscript to:

LDP: Submissions Dept
Po Box 870494
Mesquite, Tx 75187

DO NOT send original manuscript. Must be a duplicate.

Provide your synopsis and a cover letter containing your full contact information.

Thanks for considering LDP and Ca$h Presents.

<u>Coming Soon from Lock Down Publications/Ca$h Presents</u>

BOW DOWN TO MY GANGSTA

By **Ca$h**

TORN BETWEEN TWO

By **Coffee**

BLOOD STAINS OF A SHOTTA **III**

By **Jamaica**

STEADY MOBBIN **III**

By **Marcellus Allen**

BLOOD OF A BOSS **VI**

By **Askari**

LOYAL TO THE GAME **IV**

LIFE OF SIN II

By **T.J. & Jelissa**

A DOPEBOY'S PRAYER **II**

By **Eddie "Wolf" Lee**

IF LOVING YOU IS WRONG... **III**

LOVE ME EVEN WHEN IT HURTS **III**

By **Jelissa**

TRUE SAVAGE **VII**

By **Chris Green**

BLAST FOR ME **III**

DUFFLE BAG CARTEL III

By **Ghost**

ADDICTIED TO THE DRAMA **III**

By **Jamila Mathis**

LIPSTICK KILLAH **III**
Mimi
A HUSTLER'S DECEIT 3
KILL ZONE **II**
BAE BELONGS TO ME III
By **Aryanna**
THE COST OF LOYALTY **III**
By **Kweli**
SHE FELL IN LOVE WITH A REAL ONE **II**
By **Tamara Butler**
RENEGADE BOYS **III**
By **Meesha**
CORRUPTED BY A GANGSTA **IV**
By **Destiny Skai**
A GANGSTER'S CODE **III**
By **J-Blunt**
KING OF NEW YORK V
RISE TO POWER III
COKE KINGS II
By **T.J. Edwards**
GORILLAZ IN THE BAY III
De'Kari
THE STREETS ARE CALLING II
Duquie Wilson
KINGPIN KILLAZ IV
STREET KINGS 2
Hood Rich

STEADY MOBBIN' **III**

Marcellus Allen

SINS OF A HUSTLA II

ASAD

TRIGGADALE II

Elijah R. Freeman

MARRIED TO A BOSS III

By Destiny Skai & Chris Green

KINGS OF THE GAME II

Playa Ray

Available Now

RESTRAINING ORDER **I & II**

By **CA$H & Coffee**

LOVE KNOWS NO BOUNDARIES **I II & III**

By **Coffee**

RAISED AS A GOON I, II, III & IV

BRED BY THE SLUMS I, II, III

BLAST FOR ME I & II

ROTTEN TO THE CORE I III

A BRONX TALE I, II, III

DUFFEL BAG CARTEL I II

By **Ghost**

LAY IT DOWN **I & II**

LAST OF A DYING BREED

BLOOD STAINS OF A SHOTTA I & II

By **Jamaica**

LOYAL TO THE GAME

LOYAL TO THE GAME II

LOYAL TO THE GAME III

LIFE OF SIN

By **TJ & Jelissa**

BLOODY COMMAS I & II

SKI MASK CARTEL I II & III

KING OF NEW YORK I II,III IV

RISE TO POWER I II

COKE KINGS

By **T.J. Edwards**

IF LOVING HIM IS WRONG…I & II

LOVE ME EVEN WHEN IT HURTS I II

By **Jelissa**

WHEN THE STREETS CLAP BACK I & II III

By **Jibril Williams**

A DISTINGUISHED THUG STOLE MY HEART I II & III

LOVE SHOULDN'T HURT I II III

RENEGADE BOYS I & II

By **Meesha**

A GANGSTER'S CODE I &, II III

By J-Blunt

PUSH IT TO THE LIMIT

By **Bre' Hayes**

BLOOD OF A BOSS **I, II, III, IV, V**

By **Askari**

THE STREETS BLEED MURDER **I, II & III**

THE HEART OF A GANGSTA I II& III

By **Jerry Jackson**

CUM FOR ME

CUM FOR ME 2

CUM FOR ME 3

CUM FOR ME 4

An **LDP Erotica Collaboration**

BRIDE OF A HUSTLA **I II & II**

THE FETTI GIRLS **I, II& III**

CORRUPTED BY A GANGSTA I, II & III

By **Destiny Skai**

WHEN A GOOD GIRL GOES BAD

By **Adrienne**

THE COST OF LOYALTY

By Kweli

A GANGSTER'S REVENGE **I II III & IV**

THE BOSS MAN'S DAUGHTERS

THE BOSS MAN'S DAUGHTERS II

THE BOSSMAN'S DAUGHTERS III

THE BOSSMAN'S DAUGHTERS IV

THE BOSS MAN'S DAUGHTERS **V**

A SAVAGE LOVE **I & II**

BAE BELONGS TO ME I II

A HUSTLER'S DECEIT I, II, III

WHAT BAD BITCHES DO I, II, III

By **Aryanna**

Coke Kings

A KINGPIN'S AMBITON

A KINGPIN'S AMBITION **II**

I MURDER FOR THE DOUGH

By **Ambitious**

TRUE SAVAGE

TRUE SAVAGE II

TRUE SAVAGE **III**

TRUE SAVAGE **IV**

TRUE SAVAGE **V**

TRUE SAVAGE **VI**

By **Chris Green**

A DOPEBOY'S PRAYER

By **Eddie "Wolf" Lee**

THE KING CARTEL **I, II & III**

By **Frank Gresham**

THESE NIGGAS AIN'T LOYAL **I, II & III**

By **Nikki Tee**

GANGSTA SHYT **I II &III**

By **CATO**

THE ULTIMATE BETRAYAL

By **Phoenix**

BOSS'N UP **I , II & III**

By **Royal Nicole**

I LOVE YOU TO DEATH

By Destiny J

I RIDE FOR MY HITTA

I STILL RIDE FOR MY HITTA

179

By **Misty Holt**
LOVE & CHASIN' PAPER
By **Qay Crockett**
TO DIE IN VAIN
SINS OF A HUSTLA
By **ASAD**
BROOKLYN HUSTLAZ
By **Boogsy Morina**
BROOKLYN ON LOCK I & II
By **Sonovia**
GANGSTA CITY
By **Teddy Duke**
A DRUG KING AND HIS DIAMOND I & II III
A DOPEMAN'S RICHES
HER MAN, MINE'S TOO I, II
CASH MONEY HO'S
By Nicole Goosby
TRAPHOUSE KING **I II & III**
KINGPIN KILLAZ I II III
STREET KINGS
By **Hood Rich**
LIPSTICK KILLAH **I, II**
CRIME OF PASSION I & II
By **Mimi**
STEADY MOBBN' **I, II**
By **Marcellus Allen**
WHO SHOT YA **I, II**

Renta

GORILLAZ IN THE BAY **I II**

DE'KARI

TRIGGADALE

Elijah R. Freeman

GOD BLESS THE TRAPPERS I, II, III

THESE SCANDALOUS STREETS I, II, III

FEAR MY GANGSTA I, II, III

THESE STREETS DON'T LOVE NOBODY I, II

BURY ME A G I, II, III, IV, V

A GANGSTA'S EMPIRE I, II, III

Tranay Adams

THE STREETS ARE CALLING

Duquie Wilson

MARRIED TO A BOSS... I II

By Destiny Skai & Chris Green

KINGS OF THE GAME II

Playa Ray

T.J. Edwards

BOOKS BY LDP'S CEO, CA$H

<u>TRUST IN NO MAN</u>
<u>TRUST IN NO MAN 2</u>
<u>TRUST IN NO MAN 3</u>
<u>BONDED BY BLOOD</u>
<u>SHORTY GOT A THUG</u>
<u>THUGS CRY</u>
<u>THUGS CRY 2</u>
<u>THUGS CRY 3</u>
<u>TRUST NO BITCH</u>
<u>TRUST NO BITCH 2</u>
<u>TRUST NO BITCH 3</u>
<u>TIL MY CASKET DROPS</u>
<u>RESTRAINING ORDER</u>
<u>RESTRAINING ORDER 2</u>
<u>IN LOVE WITH A CONVICT</u>

<u>Coming Soon</u>
BONDED BY BLOOD 2
BOW DOWN TO MY GANGSTA

Coke Kings

www.ingramcontent.com/pod-product-compliance
Lightning Source LLC
Chambersburg PA
CBHW070522260626
47161CB00004B/1613